TITANIC

BOOK TWO

☆

COLLISION COURSE

LOOK FOR MORE ADVENTURE FROM
GORDON KORMAN

TITANIC
BOOK ONE: UNSINKABLE
BOOK TWO: COLLISION COURSE
BOOK THREE: S.O.S.

KIDNAPPED
BOOK ONE: THE ABDUCTION
BOOK TWO: THE SEARCH
BOOK THREE: THE RESCUE

ON THE RUN
BOOK ONE: CHASING THE FALCONERS
BOOK TWO: THE FUGITIVE FACTOR
BOOK THREE: NOW YOU SEE THEM, NOW YOU DON'T
BOOK FOUR: THE STOWAWAY SOLUTION
BOOK FIVE: PUBLIC ENEMIES
BOOK SIX: HUNTING THE HUNTER

DIVE
BOOK ONE: THE DISCOVERY
BOOK TWO: THE DEEP
BOOK THREE: THE DANGER

EVEREST
BOOK ONE: THE CONTEST
BOOK TWO: THE CLIMB
BOOK THREE: THE SUMMIT

ISLAND
BOOK ONE: SHIPWRECK
BOOK TWO: SURVIVAL
BOOK THREE: ESCAPE

TITANIC

BOOK TWO

COLLISION COURSE

GORDON KORMAN

SCHOLASTIC INC.

NEW YORK   TORONTO   LONDON   AUCKLAND

SYDNEY   MEXICO CITY   NEW DELHI   HONG KONG

ISBN 978-0-545-12332-7

20 19 18 17   18 19 20/0

Printed in the U.S.A.   40
First printing, August 2011

The text type was set in Sabon.
Book design by Tim Hall

FOR DAISY

CHAPTER ONE

RMS *TITANIC*
FRIDAY, APRIL 12, 1912, 4:50 P.M.

"But, Mrs. Rankin!" the steward exclaimed in confusion. "You have four sons, not five!"

Five boys, ranging in age from six years old to seventeen, lined up in descending order of height in front of the bunk beds in the narrow third-class cabin.

"I think I know my own children, Mr. Steptoe," the slight, red-haired woman replied. "Aidan, Curran, Patrick, Finnbar, and Sean — he's the wee one."

"The reason I'm asking," the steward stammered, flustered, "is Second Officer Lightoller believes there may be a stowaway on board the *Titanic* —"

"So he sent you down to the steerage, because where else could a lawbreaker be?" she finished coldly.

"I'm merely saying," Steptoe soldiered on patiently, "that it's my recollection that you boarded in Queenstown with your *four* sons — three here in the cabin with you, and your older boy in the forward berths, with the single men."

"Then your recollection is wrong." Mrs. Rankin may have been small, but raising a family by herself in County Kilkenny had made her tough. "I may not be a millionaire like your John Jacob Astor up in first class, but you have no right to interrogate me in the peace of my own cabin."

"Madam, your stubbornness would be astonishing in the most obstinate mule!" The steward's face was red with frustration. "I shall return with the passenger manifest and prove that I am right!" He stormed out, slamming the hatch behind him.

Paddy Burns, age fourteen, stepped out of the line of boys. He was fair of complexion, and dressed like the younger Rankins, in a plain work shirt, breeches, and knee socks. But he was not one of them. Was it really only ten days ago that he had been living on the streets of Belfast, picking pockets to survive? The great *Titanic* had been nothing more than an immense form under construction in a slip at Harland and Wolff. The four towering smokestacks had cast shadows over Paddy, Daniel, and half the city.

Daniel, the best friend a lad could ever have. Dead because of my mistake . . .

He shook his head to clear it. All the sorrow in the

world wouldn't bring Daniel back. Besides, it wasn't the Rankins' problem. The family had risked a lot to protect Paddy from the crew. Harboring a stowaway was a serious crime.

"That steward will be back, he will," Paddy fretted. "And he'll bring the passenger records to *prove* how many there are in your party."

Mrs. Rankin was unworried. "We'll tell him he must be soft in the head, because that's what we've been saying all along. *He* was the one who had it backward."

"But —"

She awarded him a motherly smile. "We Irish haven't survived all these years under the English because we're stupid and weak."

Paddy nodded slowly. "First the clothes, and now protecting me — I don't know how I'll ever repay you."

"You'll repay me by making a life for yourself in America," she assured him. "The English can steal our crops and tell us there's a famine. But our spirit — *that* they'll never take, not even with their soldiers and their guns. Now off you go, before Mr. High and Mighty comes back."

Paddy stepped out into the third-class passageway. In the days since he'd become an accidental stowaway aboard the *Titanic*, he'd explored every inch of the magnificent vessel. Steerage was not nearly as opulent and luxurious as first class or even second. But the entire ship was brand new — clean and freshly painted. And, he reflected ruefully, he'd only seen a grand total of three rats — far fewer than he and Daniel had chased out of the abandoned print shop they had made their home back in Belfast.

Belfast. It already seemed a million miles away, and a hundred years ago.

Make a life for yourself. . . . Mrs. Rankin's words echoed in his mind. Did Paddy even deserve a life after what his heedlessness had done to Daniel? Perhaps not. But the world continued to turn, and the ship continued to sail. He had to live in the here and now, not in the past. If surviving made little sense, the alternative made that much less.

So, to the matter at hand. He needed somewhere to go — a place where Lightoller and the other officers would not find him.

But first he had an errand to run.

He found a companion stairway that led up to E Deck, and hurried forward along the wide corridor nicknamed Scotland Road.

As he walked past crew members, he fancied that their eyes were scanning him. It made him nervous. But, he reasoned, the stowaway had been last seen wearing a steward's uniform. Clothed as a third-class boy, he should be safe enough — unless he ran into Lightoller or one of the sailors who had seen him up close.

He rounded the corner and approached the office of the master-at-arms. Word had traveled around the ship that two second-class passengers had been locked in the brig for attempted murder, most foul. Paddy knew all about it, because he was the one who had nearly been killed.

Flattening himself to the bulkhead, he peered in through the doorway. The desk was deserted. Boldly, he took a step inside and turned to face the detention cells.

There they were: Kevin Gilhooley, brother of the most powerful gangster in Belfast, and beside him, a hulking bodyguard with a thrice-broken nose, Seamus.

"You look good behind bars," Paddy said with satisfaction. These were the two who had killed Daniel, and had recently tried to pitch Paddy off the top deck of the *Titanic*.

"You're a lucky little rat — I'll give you that," growled Gilhooley. "But luck won't stop this boat from reaching New York. And then you're mine."

"And mine," added Seamus in a nasal voice.

Paddy stuck his jaw out defiantly. "You'll never touch me! You're going to jail for what you did!"

"You think the Americans will be interested in what happened aboard a ship half a world away?" Gilhooley shook his head. "Enjoy your sweet voyage, boy. Use their gymnasium and have yourself a real Turkish steam bath. Because when I get my hands on you, you're going to squeal like your little friend in the Belfast shipyards."

To hear Kevin Gilhooley talking about Daniel's murder — *bragging* about it — turned Paddy's rational thoughts into a blind rage. He snatched the pitcher of ice water from the desk and flung it at the cell.

There was a crash as the glass shattered against the bars, sloshing a torrent of water and broken shards over Gilhooley. The shocked howl that exploded from the gangster's throat came as much from the icy deluge as from anger at Paddy.

"Guard!"

Paddy darted out of the office, moving away from Scotland Road, where crew members were sure to hear Gilhooley's bellowing and come running. He hurried up a small companion staircase past D Deck to C and paused, catching his breath.

A well-dressed gentleman in a dark suit shot him a disapproving glance as he walked by.

He was in first class now — he could tell by the luxurious thickness of the carpeting, the paneled walls, and gleaming brass fixtures. Dressed like a common urchin from steerage, he stood out like a sore thumb.

Third-class passengers were not allowed in this domain of millionaires. That made no difference to Paddy — strictly speaking, he wasn't allowed *anywhere*. Still, if he were caught and questioned, sooner or later someone would realize that he and the mysterious stowaway happened to be one and the same.

He had to get out of here. But where could he go? He couldn't head below. At that very moment, a search party could be forming on E Deck. And going up would only bring him farther into the rarefied air of first class.

He caught a flash of navy blue at the end of the passageway — the color of the officers' uniforms. Paddy froze. Lightoller?

No, but not much better — Fifth Officer Lowe, known for his megaphone voice and firecracker temper.

Paddy looked around desperately. The corridor

offered no hiding places, only solid bulkheads and locked staterooms.

In the opposite direction down the hall, a maid was wheeling a canvas bin, collecting linens. He watched as she knocked on a cabin door, opened it with a passkey, and disappeared inside.

The decision was made in the blink of an eye. Paddy sprinted along the passageway and dove into the cart, burrowing deep into a collection of large, thirsty bath towels. A moment later, the maid emerged. A few more towels were tossed on top, and the cart began to roll again.

He held his breath, waiting for the sound of pounding feet on the carpet. Then his cover would be cast aside, and Lowe would be glaring down at him. . . .

It didn't happen. The hamper stopped. More linens were added, and they were moving once more.

He shifted his position and felt a corner of folded paper scratch against his skin. He had doggedly held the drawing to his chest ever since Belfast. He was not at all certain why. He both loved and hated this weathered page. Loved it because it had come from Daniel. Hated it because it had cost Daniel his life.

Mr. Thomas Andrews himself — creator of this great ship — had challenged Daniel to imagine a way the unsinkable *Titanic* might sink. And Daniel had succeeded! At least, Paddy thought he had. Try as he might, Paddy could not make head or tail of his friend's strange sketch. Daniel had been so much more than the street lad that fate had made him. He was cleverer than the designers and engineers who built ocean liners.

Paddy's thoughts darkened. Daniel had been murdered while trying to deliver this drawing to Mr. Andrews. And in that way, Paddy cursed it — just as he cursed himself for bringing Kevin Gilhooley down upon them.

Paddy's reverie was interrupted by the rattle of a gate, followed by the maid's voice: "B Deck, please." And then they were rising.

Paddy had never been on a real electric elevator before this voyage, but it was a common thing for the *Titanic*'s passengers. The liner had three of them.

So he was away from Fifth Officer Lowe. It was good news, but it also introduced a larger problem. Up here, in the heart of first class, how was he ever going to get out of this linen bin?

He was trapped in the lap of luxury.

CHAPTER TWO

RMS *TITANIC*
FRIDAY, APRIL 12, 1912, 5:05 P.M.

"Don't mind the cold, my dears! The stimulation of physical exercise will soon warm your bones!"

Major Mountjoy's ample belly wobbled with each step as he set up the ringtoss game on a wide part of the A-Deck promenade.

Sophie Bronson and Juliana Glamm exchanged dubious glances. How much physical exercise could they expect from Major Muttonchop, their dinner tablemate and quite possibly the most boring person aboard the RMS *Titanic*? Sometimes it seemed as if he intended to spend the entire voyage tracking them like a bloodhound. Sophie and Juliana were equally determined to avoid the man.

"Well, let's get on with it," Sophie announced with a sigh. "Those rings aren't going to toss themselves."

She caught a sharp look from her friend, who was an earl's daughter, and more accustomed to the old-fashioned ways of society. Sophie was an American girl, very much in the new twentieth century. She got this from her mother, who was modern in her thinking. Too modern, some would say. But that was another story.

"Quite right!" the major blustered through his bright-red side whiskers. "The key to success at ring toss is a combination of arm speed and keenness of eye. There is no strength involved; it is pure skill."

Sighting like a marksman, he leaned forward and launched his ring. It landed on edge and rolled like a hoop, coming to rest against the half wall that semi-enclosed the promenade. Had it not been for the abutment, it would have wound up in the sea.

"Nice shot," Sophie commented blandly.

Juliana took a ring and awaited her turn. Major Mountjoy did not move, but stayed frozen in his follow-through position.

"Are you all right, Major?" she asked solicitously.

"I seem to have done myself an injury," Mountjoy replied in a strained voice. "It happened during the Boer War, in a cavalry charge outside Jo'burg. I was in charge of a brigade then, you see. . . ."

It boggled the imagination, Sophie reflected. Even doubled over in pain, Major Muttonchop could still come up with a long, dreary story. All the way down to the hospital on D Deck, he rambled on about his exploits in South Africa. His posture may have been locked at a right angle, but his mouth was in perfect form.

"Shed no tears for me, my dears," he called as they made their escape. "I shall be right as rain in no time. I've had this crooked back since that cavalry charge outside Jo'burg. . . ."

The story restarted, this time aimed at Dr. O'Loughlin, the *Titanic*'s surgeon.

The giggling began on the elevator.

"Sophie!" Juliana hissed. "It's not seemly to laugh like a hyena in public."

"I'm not laughing," Sophie gurgled, barely under control. "I'm shedding tears for the major."

That set Juliana off. And by the time the girls let themselves into Juliana's stateroom, B-56, they were both shedding tears for Major Muttonchop — tears of mirth.

"If he got the wonky back on a cavalry charge," Sophie managed, "think of the wonky back on the poor horse that was carrying him!"

"How long has he been pleading for the honor of teaching us the fine points of ringtoss?" Juliana added. "And then, on his very first throw —"

She fell silent, frowning. The suite was as beautifully

appointed as any chamber in any manor house in England, with elegant furniture, silk wallpaper, velvet drapery, and a vaulted ceiling. Every detail was perfect down to the tiniest tassel on the Persian rug in the sitting room.

So why was a stack of blankets piled haphazardly on Juliana's canopy bed?

"This isn't the level of service one would expect of the White Star Line," she said disapprovingly. "I shall ring for a steward at once."

"Julie," Sophie chided, "why drag some poor fellow away from his tea break? In half the time it would take for him to come calling, you and I could set everything right." She bent down to the captain's drawer built into the bed and pulled on the handle. Her brow furrowed. "It's stuck."

She grabbed on with two hands and yanked with all her might. The chest lurched open, and she cried out in shock. There, his knees drawn to his chest in the tight space, lay Paddy Burns.

"I can explain —" he began.

"Paddy, what are you doing in first class?" Juliana blurted.

Paddy bristled, and Sophie could see why. Here he was, a stowaway, hunted by the White Star Line and, up until a few hours ago, ruthless gangsters. And what was Julie's reaction to finding him skulking in the furniture? What was his business amid the nobility and high society of the *Titanic*'s upper decks?

"Well, I was in the neighborhood, so I thought I'd pop in for a spot of tea," Paddy told Juliana in his best English accent, which wasn't very English at all.

Sophie played the role of peacemaker. "She means why are you in her stateroom — and in the drawer, of all places?"

Stepping gingerly out of his hiding place, Paddy recounted the story of his visit to the brig, and how the laundry cart had provided his getaway. "By the time it was safe to climb out of there, I was all the way up on B Deck. I recognized your stateroom, and I thought —" He studied his battered hobnail boots on the lustrous carpet. "Well, miss, you were kind enough to help me the last time —"

"But how did you get *inside*?" Juliana persisted. "The suite was locked."

"Ah, the lock." Paddy produced a small hairpin from the pocket of his breeches. "Begging your pardon, but I don't see what all the fuss is about."

There was a click, and the door of stateroom B-56 swung wide.

"Julie?" queried the voice of the seventeenth Earl of Glamford.

"My father!" Juliana hissed urgently.

Before Paddy could respond, Sophie pushed him back down into the drawer and slammed the captain's bed shut.

"Hello, Papa." Juliana stepped into the doorway in an attempt to block the goings-on with her slender figure. "How was your card game?"

"Excellent," he replied briskly, although his sour expression and the dark circles beneath his eyes told a different story. The earl's fondness for gaming was exceeded only by his lack of skill at it. Nowhere was the situation more dangerous than on a long ocean voyage. There was an abundance of wealthy players and precious little else for them to do.

He looked beyond his daughter to Sophie in the bedchamber. "Miss Bronson," he acknowledged with barely a nod.

"Your Lordship," Sophie said, nodding back. *Uh-oh*, she thought. He seemed to be slurring his words. Julie had said that her father drank when he was losing at cards. More likely, he lost at cards because he was drinking. There was an expansive light-brown stain on his shirt. Liquor. She was sure of it.

His bleary eyes shifted from Sophie to the linens piled on the bed. "What on earth? Am I to assume that the chambermaid left those? Ring for the steward at once! When I travel first class, I expect it to be so."

"Oh, Papa," Juliana giggled. "It's but the work of a moment to set it right."

"You forget your position, young lady," the earl said sternly. "*You* are not the chambermaid. You are the daughter of a peer, and you would do well to remember it."

Juliana dropped her gaze. "Is there something I can do for you, Papa? You don't normally leave the lounge so early."

"I came to change my shirt. I spilled — tea all down the front. Walmsley will be here directly to assist me."

The girls exchanged a worried glance. If Walmsley the valet didn't get here soon, Paddy was going to suffocate in that drawer!

"You are no longer a child, Julie," the earl went on. "Do you think I don't notice how you fraternize with that Alfie boy?"

"He's our steward!" Juliana protested, shocked.

"I'm delighted that you know it. You are a member of a family that stretches back for centuries. Your position is hardly enhanced by such an acquaintance."

Stung, Juliana dared to strike back. "I'm impressed that you observe so much from a card table in the lounge."

Sophie was amazed that tradition-bound Juliana would stand up to her father in this manner. At that, she was less surprised than the earl himself.

He was just about to rattle the walls with his outrage when Walmsley let himself in, bearing a selection of fresh shirts from the laundry. The valet and his master retired to the other bedchamber and shut the door behind them.

In a flash, the girls pulled open the drawer and helped Paddy out.

"Quickly," Juliana whispered. "You need to leave before my father finishes dressing!"

Paddy looked at her, eyes wide. "Your father is a proper piece of goods, he is! He speaks to you like no loving parent."

"How dare you!" Juliana demanded. "He is protecting my reputation, as is his responsibility."

"Is that how you explain it to yourself?" he asked cynically. "Maybe I wasn't born in your mansions, but even a poor boy has a nose. I can tell when something smells, I can."

"What are you insinuating?" Juliana's voice grew shrill.

"To your high-and-mighty father, a junior steward is something to be used, like a cane or a footstool. All that blather about your reputation — what I'm saying, miss, is there's something not quite right about it."

"You are speaking of the Earl of Glamford!" Juliana seethed. "You will show him the respect he is due."

"I am," Paddy said simply.

"Would you two stop bickering?" Sophie broke in. "What are we going to do with Paddy? We have to get him out of first class!"

"I can't go back to steerage," Paddy told them. "The crew is looking for me there."

From the master suite, the earl's voice could be heard. "A fresh cravat, Walmsley. Before I miss another round."

"We'll find Alfie," Juliana decided. "He'll know what to do."

CHAPTER THREE

RMS *TITANIC*
FRIDAY, APRIL 12, 1912, 5:35 P.M.

Number 5 Boiler Room was so hot that Alfie half expected the wool of his steward's jacket to burst into flames. He felt a wave of pity as he regarded his father, black with coal dust, glistening with sweat, plying his shovel. The stokers of the *Titanic*'s black gang lived and worked far below the waterline in a sunken realm of darkness and fire.

"Aye, boy," John Huggins was telling his son. "Captain Smith gave the order this morning to light two more boilers."

"I don't know how you stand it, Da," Alfie gasped, running a finger under his tight collar.

His father grinned. "I won't lie to you. There are times when I go up on deck for a breather and I'm sore tempted to take a swim over the side, just to cool down. Then I remember how cold that ocean is, and I'm proper grateful to be hot again."

"Why do they need more boilers?" Alfie questioned.

John Huggins shrugged. "If you want your horse to go faster, you give him a bigger pail of oats. If you want more speed, you pour on more coal. She's making better than five hundred miles a day — well better, I'd wager. I've never worked a finer ship."

Alfie looked nervous. "Five hundred miles a day! Is that even safe?"

His father laughed. "We're in the middle of the Atlantic. The fish don't care how fast we pass by. We've two more burners yet to light. I expect that order will come tomorrow sometime. There's talk of making New York by Tuesday night, half a day ahead of schedule. Wouldn't that be something?"

"I suppose," Alfie agreed, bewildered. "But what's the advantage of steaming into New York Harbor in the wee hours? The passengers will be asleep, and so will the city they're landing in."

"The newspapers, lad," the fireman explained. "The maiden voyage of the greatest ship ever built! When the papers come out Wednesday morning, the name *Titanic* should be in every headline, in the largest type!"

"John!" came a bellow that cut through the clamor of the boiler room. A sailor appeared partway down the ladder from the upper decks. "Is your boy there with you?"

Alfie moved to the foot of the ladder. "I'm right here."

"A passenger wants you."

"I'm off duty," Alfie protested.

The man laughed. "Well, get back *on* duty. Miss Glamm needs a hat from the baggage hold."

Alfie was mystified. "Miss Glamm? What hat? She has more hats than I have hairs on my head."

"Or you can ignore her and hear about it from Mr. Lightoller. It's up to you." And he was gone.

"Better go, lad," his father called good-naturedly. "You know these first-class ladies and their frills and fancies."

Alfie walked forward, ducking through the hatch that separated the boiler rooms from the fireman's passage that led to the holds in the ship's bow. At the touch of a single button on the bridge, a watertight door would come down and seal that opening. There were fifteen such doors dividing the hull of the *Titanic* into closed compartments. This was the feature that made her unsinkable. In the unlikely event that anything pierced the double steel hull, the flooding could be instantly and completely contained.

In the passage, the temperature dropped appreciably. That, at least, was a relief. But the prospect of spending the rest of his afternoon off running hatboxes up and down the spiral staircase to Juliana was not very appealing.

As a stoker's son, Alfie had met very few wealthy people prior to this voyage. It was astonishing how a change of hat could be so important to the captains of government and industry who determined the fate of the world. Giants obsessed with nonsense.

Still, he was puzzled that Juliana would call him rather than the steward on duty. She was a fancy lady, yes, but usually considerate. She knew that Alfie valued his visits with his father now that Mum had abandoned them.

He stopped in his tracks, suddenly overcome by loneliness for his mother. He felt no anger toward her. He even understood a little why she might run away from her drab life. Mum was a dreamer, her nose forever buried in a penny novel. What else did he expect from a woman who had named her only son Alphonse after the hero in her favorite French romance? To be the wife of John Huggins — who was away at sea far longer than he was ever at home — must have been unbearable for her.

Stop feeling sorry for yourself! Alfie thought. *There are many whose lot is far worse than your own.*

After all, his scheme had worked perfectly. He had lied about his age and signed on with the White Star Line so he and Da could sail together. They were aboard the *Titanic*, the finest ship in the world. He was *lucky*.

He opened the hatch to the baggage hold and stepped inside, surveying the vast landscape of crates, trunks, and suitcases, all secured by netting. High society did not travel light. Some of the first-class staterooms had stashed as many as forty pieces of luggage.

At least he didn't have to search for Juliana's things. Alfie had spent a lot of time in the hold. He already knew where to find the Glamm baggage — closer to the spiral staircase, not far from the Astors' vast collection of trunks and boxes.

He stiffened at the sound of a footfall close behind him. But when he wheeled around, there was no one there.

Frowning now, he faced up to Juliana's hatboxes, stacked higher than he was tall. Now, which one of these could possibly be the one she wanted? And how was he to know, by the way?

A cat meowed somewhere behind the Astors' luggage. Alfie knew there was at least one on board, kept in the stewardesses' quarters. But when he looked behind the pile, there was no sign of the animal.

A deep unease gripped him. He had reason to believe that there was a criminal on board, a notorious murderer from long ago. Could this man be stalking him?

He felt hot breath on the back of his neck.

CHAPTER FOUR

RMS *TITANIC*
FRIDAY, APRIL 12, 1912, 5:55 P.M.

Terrified, Alfie spun on his heel. The figure was so close that it took a moment for him to focus and recognize who was standing there.

"Paddy!" he wheezed.

The young stowaway was bent over double with laughter. "If only you could have seen the look upon your face!"

"You fool! I might have done you a serious injury!"

Paddy, who had survived a year on the streets of Belfast, was unperturbed. "How does your being frightened harm me?"

"Don't be cute!" Alfie rasped. "I could have screamed my head off and brought half the crew down on us. What are you doing here, anyway? I thought we agreed you were going to hide in steerage."

"I can't stay there anymore," Paddy replied. "Their stewards can count, same as in first and second class. One of them remembered how many sons Mrs. Rankin came aboard with. She wasn't inclined to part with one of her own, you see. So here I am. A long story, it is, but Miss Fancy Pants sent me down to wait for you." He flashed Alfie a cheeky grin. "You needn't bother with the hatboxes."

Alfie groaned. "What am I going to do with you, Paddy? You know you're not safe in the hold."

Paddy shrugged. "I'm not safe anywhere. This place is no worse and no better." He locked earnest eyes on Alfie's. "Don't you worry. If I'm found, I'll not tell them who helped me — neither you nor the girls."

"You can't let yourself get arrested! They'll put you in the brig with those Gilhooley monsters!"

"Maybe not," Paddy reasoned. "The captain knows they tried to murder me."

"Do you think the White Star Line cares what happens to a stowaway? Mr. Lightoller will be more than happy to let those gangsters finish the job they started!"

"Then I won't get caught," Paddy said stubbornly. "If the officers get too close, I'll just move on. I did it in Belfast. I can do it here."

Alfie shook his head. "Not all day and all night. Everybody has to sleep. Even you."

Paddy nodded reluctantly. "You have the right of it. So where does a desperate fugitive lay his head for a few hours to gather strength for the next chase?" He looked around, his bright gaze coming to rest on an enormous steamer trunk. "Would you take a gander at that! It's easily the size of a small bedchamber."

Alfie was horrified. "What are you thinking? That luggage belongs to John Jacob Astor!"

"The richest man in the world can well afford to lend me the use of it for a few days." Paddy slithered under the netting and attacked the brass lock with the hairpin he'd used to gain access to suite B-56. It took about seven seconds before the lid was open and he was examining the contents.

The trunk was piled high with the most luxurious silks and satin brocades — fabrics purchased by the famous couple in Europe and Egypt to have made into clothing back in the United States.

"This'll be a nice, soft bed," Paddy decided. "Now for some air holes."

"Paddy, there's a difference between kipping in some wealthy man's trunk and making holes in it!"

"Merely small ones," Paddy promised. "By the hinges in the back, where they won't be noticed." He inserted the hairpin in the joints, working the narrow metal in a small circle to create some separation. "That should do it. Now I just have to remove some of this stuff so I fit." He grabbed an armload of silky material.

"Be careful with that!" Alfie moaned. "It probably costs more than you and I will ever touch in our whole lives."

"Would I deprive a millionaire of his fancy rags? I'm folding it beautifully, I am. And I'll put it right into one of his other bags."

He held up a large leather case. All at once, the piece fell open, broken, and out showered books, clothing, and a single torn leaf of heavy yellowed paper.

Scrapbook paper.

Alfie flattened himself to the floor and scrambled under the netting to join Paddy with the Astor luggage. The two stared at the ripped sheet and then at each other.

They had seen this paper before, and in this very baggage compartment. The scrapbook it had come from had been loose in the hold. Its pages chronicled grisly crimes from twenty-four years before — the Whitechapel murders. The killer, known only as Jack the Ripper, had never been caught or even identified.

The scrapbook held old newspaper broadsheets and notes that could only have been written by one person — Jack the Ripper himself. Worse, there were "souvenirs" from the victims — bloodstained fabric, earrings, even human teeth and skin.

Still pasted to the paper were a few links of an inexpensive bracelet above a handwritten notation:

Approached from the rear, struck swiftly.

The formation of the letters was a perfect match for the writing they had seen in the scrapbook.

"But —" Paddy was thunderstruck. "This is the *Astors'* luggage!"

"I don't think so," Alfie told him, round-eyed. "Look — the Astor trunks all match, except for this one. What if the porters broke this bag and hid it to avoid getting into trouble?" He examined the luggage tag, which proclaimed that this leather bag belonged to the occupant of stateroom A-17.

"So you're saying that the person in A-17 — that's Jack the Ripper?" asked Paddy.

Alfie set his jaw grimly. "I've got to go back and take my passengers to dinner. But don't worry. I'll find him."

CHAPTER FIVE

The *Titanic*'s first-class dining saloon was the largest and most luxurious room aboard any ship anywhere. It sat more than five hundred people in glorious Jacobean splendor, ablaze in the electric light.

For the first time, table 22 had a full complement of diners, including Juliana's father, the earl, and Sophie's mother, Amelia Bronson, the noted suffragist.

Major Mountjoy was there, too. Thanks to the talents of the ship's surgeon, he was no longer bent at a right angle, but at a more relaxed 135 degrees. He sat there like an oriental potentate, propped up by many pillows. And as usual, he provided most of the conversation.

"My word! I am bowed down with grief that I was

unable to complete my instructions to the two young ladies."

The earl raised melancholy bloodshot eyes from the contemplation of his hand, where there were, alas, no cards. "What are you talking about? What instructions?"

"Papa," Juliana explained patiently, "the major was kind enough to be showing us the fine points of ringtoss when he injured his back."

Amelia Bronson spoke up in the sharp, no-nonsense voice that was natural to her. "Tell me, Major: Is it because you happen to be a man that you are instantly qualified to dispense lessons on a pointless skill that could be learned by any half-intelligent baboon?"

"Mother —" Sophie began warningly. Her mother's speechmaking and activism often landed her under arrest and even in jail. These were the moments that Sophie dreaded the most. The dining saloon was such a beautiful, festive place. Why couldn't Mother simply enjoy the magnificent meal instead of scoring points for women's rights? Major Muttonchop may have been as tiresome as he was rotund, but he was a nice man who didn't deserve to be skewered by a woman with a tongue like a razor-sharp sword.

More embarrassing still was Amelia Bronson's choice of clothing. She wore exclusively purple, white, and green, the colors of the suffragist movement. Here they were, among the wealthiest, most celebrated people alive, and Mother looked like she was draped in the flag of some exotic banana republic.

Luckily, Major Mountjoy was not offended by his tablemate's harsh words. "Well met, Mrs. Bronson. Very well met, indeed. I happen to be a staunch supporter of votes for women. It would definitely pretty up those polling stations. Such drab, dreary places."

Amelia Bronson said nothing, but her eyes burned. Being considered merely decorative was almost as bad as being denied the vote.

Anxious for a change of subject, Sophie glanced expectantly at a passing waiter. The elegance and beauty of the room was exceeded only by the sheer volume of fine food served there. Dinner in first class stretched for twelve or thirteen courses and always ended with a dessert from Henri Jaillet, the renowned pastry chef. (Last night it had been chocolate mousse napoleons, each piece a work of art.) The diners were the pampered of the world, used to the very best of everything. And they got it here.

When the lights dimmed in the saloon, excitement

buzzed in the vast room. Never mind that every single diner was already full to bursting. The anticipation of the next marvelous dessert was all that was required to give them an appetite.

An army of waiters marched in from the kitchen, bearing huge platters of cherries jubilee flambé. There were oohs and aahs, and even a sprinkling of applause. The flaming brandy cast a bluish glow on the white walls and the gentlemen's gleaming starched shirtfronts.

When the tray tipped and the burning dessert slid onto table 23, the fine linen cloth ignited almost immediately. There were screams as the flames shot toward the ceiling. In the mad scramble to evacuate the nearby tables, the earl took Juliana's hand and spirited her out of harm's way.

Sophie reached for her mother's arm and found that Amelia Bronson was no longer beside her.

"Mother?"

"*Stand back!*" bellowed a strident female voice.

Mrs. Bronson charged through the chaos, her gown hiked up as she hauled a heavy extinguisher to the scene of the fire. Two huge leaps brought her first onto a chair, and then atop the table itself. With a gargantuan effort, she upended the extinguisher and pressed the nozzle.

The explosion of chemical foam was sudden and violent, but Mrs. Bronson never wavered. Within seconds, a mountain of lather covered the tabletop, and the fire was out.

Still brandishing the metal tank, she stood there, hair hanging down in wet strings, her purple, white, and green evening gown soaked in foam.

Total silence fell in the saloon. Even the musicians put down their instruments and stared.

Captain E. J. Smith, resplendent in his white dress uniform, approached the wreckage. "Magnificent, madam. This vessel owes you a debt of gratitude."

Sophie knew all too well what was coming next. As the excitement of the moment faded, Amelia Bronson would realize that, in a way, she was in a very familiar place — standing on a raised platform, surrounded by an audience. She was not going to pass up the chance to speak her mind in front of some of the most influential people on two continents.

"Take a look at the men!" she challenged in ringing tones. "Where are our husbands and fathers, whom we trust to shape the world? Cowering in corners! Lying on the deck! Tiptoeing for the exits! I stand before you, a woman — one of half the population not trusted to make the decisions affecting our lives. And I say: Had I not made *this* decision — to act — this beautiful dining room might well lie in charred ruins! *Votes for women!*" she bellowed, trying to start a chant.

Her words echoed off silent walls.

"Quite right," said Captain Smith with much less warmth and enthusiasm. He held out his arm, but she made a point of jumping down without his assistance.

"Votes for women," she muttered, glaring at the female faces. "Even the ones who don't help the cause."

Sophie had to turn away to hide her humiliation.

The earl patted Sophie's hand sympathetically. "My poor girl, we cannot choose our relatives."

"Perhaps Mrs. Bronson isn't entirely wrong," Juliana pointed out thoughtfully. "She alone had the presence of mind to fetch the extinguisher, while the men —" Her eyes fell on a white-haired gentleman who was sprawled on the floor beside his overturned chair. He was reaching for his crutch, which had landed just beyond his grasp. "Captain!" she exclaimed. "Someone must help him!"

Captain Smith and a waiter assisted the man to his feet and restored the crutch to its place under his arm. The captain motioned for a steward, and Alfie stepped forward.

"Accompany Mr. Masterson to his cabin and see to it that he is comfortable."

"Yes, sir." Alfie positioned himself at Mr. Masterson's free arm and offered his support. "Easy does it, sir. We'll go out to the lift and get you home all right and tight."

Masterson cast him a sour look. "I'm lame in the legs, boy, not the head. You're not talking to a child."

By the time the two limped out of the dining saloon, the ruined table had been whisked away and replaced with a spotless new one. The waiters were serving the cherries jubilee, minus the fire. And the orchestra was once again playing dinner music. Silverware began to clink against fine china.

"You needn't trouble yourself," Mr. Masterson told Alfie impatiently in the passageway. "I can manage well enough on my own."

"It's no trouble at all, sir," Alfie said cheerfully. "I'm happy to be of service."

"Oh, well, as long as *you're* happy," Masterson growled. "Did anybody ask me if *I'm* happy?"

"Now, sir," Alfie soothed. "The order came from Captain Smith himself."

Mr. Masterson was unimpressed. "That overstuffed popinjay?"

"Sir! Captain Smith is the commodore of the White

Star Line, the most experienced sea captain in the world!"

The white-haired man leaned on his crutch and peered at Alfie critically. "How long have *you* been a sailor? Ten seconds?"

Alfie's face burned. Was his inexperience so obvious? "This is my first voyage," he admitted.

"I never would have guessed," Mr. Masterson said sarcastically. "A Deck," he barked to the elevator operator.

"Did you have a pleasant dinner, sir?" the young man asked.

"Oh, splendid. I was almost set ablaze, and then some crazed Amazon made a speech about votes for women. As if *that* could ever happen. Lord, save us!"

Once on A Deck, Masterson thumped on his crutch with such great speed that Alfie had to scramble to keep up with him.

The older man fumbled with his keys and let himself into the stateroom.

"Would you like me to come in, sir?" Alfie offered. "I could assist you —"

Slam! The door shut, nearly taking off the tip of Alfie's nose.

Alfie tried to think charitable thoughts about a poor crippled man. But all that came to mind was:

What kind of miserable person treats a servant this way?

And then his eyes focused on the brass plaque that identified the stateroom number.

A-17.

He had a brief vision of a baggage tag and a ghastly piece of scrapbook paper.

Mr. Masterson was Jack the Ripper.

CHAPTER SIX

RMS *TITANIC*
SATURDAY, APRIL 13, 1912, 7:05 A.M.

Sleeping in the Astors' trunk was like being laid out in a coffin when you were still alive. Paddy did not like it one little bit.

It was comfortable enough. Never again was he going to be wrapped in such luxurious fabrics. But being closed in a box made him think about dying, and that made him think about Daniel.

The whole point of setting up this trunk was so he could have a safe place to sleep. And the fact was he was hardly sleeping at all. He would toss and turn, dozing no more than a few minutes at a time. When he did finally drop off, he would awake gasping for breath and choking over the sickly sweet smell of the perfumed sachets placed among the linens.

When Alfie threw open the lid of the trunk early the next morning, Paddy felt more tired than when he'd laid down his head the night before.

"I brought you some breakfast." The young steward pulled a fresh scone out of each pocket of his jacket. "Sorry I couldn't make away with any tea."

"This is fine!" Paddy ate hungrily. One thing life in Belfast had taught him: You never turned your nose up at food, even if you were too exhausted to be hungry.

Alfie was bursting with excitement. "I found him!"

"Found who?" Paddy opened his eyes wide. "Not Jack the Ripper?"

"His name is Robert Masterson," Alfie supplied breathlessly, "and he's staying in A-17. I checked the passenger manifest. No wife, no valet. He's the only one in that stateroom. It's impossible for the scrapbook to belong to anybody but him!"

Paddy chewed thoughtfully. "And you're certain that your suspicion is true?"

"Masterson is lame in both legs. That explains why the Whitechapel murders suddenly stopped. Once he could barely walk, he was no longer able to chase down his victims on dark streets. And no wonder Jack the Ripper was never caught. Why would the police suspect a cripple?"

"You'd better be *really* sure," Paddy said slowly. "He's a proper first-class toff, he is. And you? You're nobody. If you accuse him and you're wrong, you'll never work on another ship. They might even clap you in irons!"

Alfie's confidence melted away. "I know I'm right. But to say all this to the captain —"

"Perhaps it's just too soon," Paddy suggested. "We've four more days before we reach America. Stay close to the man. Befriend him. Maybe you'll find proof positive."

"You have no idea what you're asking," Alfie groaned. "He's a horrible, nasty, unbearable person!"

"Did you expect him to be sweet and agreeable?" Paddy demanded impatiently. "He's Jack the Ripper!"

"Even if I could tolerate his company, he hates me. All I did was help him to his cabin on the captain's direct order. He heaped abuse upon me every step of the way. He won't accept my friendship. He'll send me away."

Paddy shrugged. "You're a steward; he's a passenger. It's your job to attend to him. You just have to find a way."

☆

Alfie returned to cabin A-17 to find Junior Steward Jules Tryhorn removing the breakfast dishes.

"Mr. Masterson is in the gymnasium," Tryhorn told Alfie. "He always takes breakfast in his stateroom, and then I escort him to the boat deck for his exercise session."

Alfie was surprised. "He can exercise in his condition?"

Tryhorn sighed. "Do I look like his physician? I drop him off at nine o'clock; I retrieve him at ten. That's all I know."

"Would you mind if I picked him up today?"

"Oh, would you?" The steward was pathetically grateful. "He doesn't seem to like me at all."

"He doesn't like me any better," Alfie admitted. "But I'll look after him for the present."

The gymnasium was located on the boat deck on the starboard side. Like many features of the *Titanic*, it was considered the largest and most modern exercise facility afloat. The polished hardwood floor gleamed with reflected light from eight huge windows. The ocean view was nothing short of spectacular, but the handful of passengers seemed intent on exercise rather than sightseeing. Alfie noticed young Mrs. Astor, just a few years older than he was himself, rowing atop the mechanical camel, her long skirts covering most of the apparatus.

She wouldn't look so carefree if she knew that a stowaway was sleeping on her fancy linens, he thought, unsure whether the idea made him want to laugh or cry.

Then his eyes fell on Mr. Masterson. He was stationed between parallel bars, raising and lowering his body with power and control. His legs might have been rubber, but his upper body was muscular and agile. His crutch, unneeded here, was propped against the wood-paneled bulkhead beneath a framed map of the world.

The gym instructor sidled up to Alfie. "Surprising, isn't it? Elsewhere, he can barely get around on his own, but look at him now."

Alfie was thinking the same thing, but with a darker twist. Suddenly, it was easy to imagine Mr. Masterson overpowering and murdering healthy women in the prime of their lives. With his hobbled legs out of the equation, he seemed more than capable of the terrible crimes of Jack the Ripper twenty-four years ago.

"He's quite . . ." — the young steward hesitated — "*fit* for someone in his condition."

The instructor nodded. "It's said that when you lose one part of the body, the others become enhanced to compensate for it. I've known strongmen who didn't have arms like that."

Yet as Mr. Masterson lowered himself down from the bars, the transformation was immediate and dramatic. When his feet touched the deck, his shoulders sagged, and his entire body seemed to collapse in upon itself.

The instructor rushed over to take his arm, but Masterson shook him off angrily. "If I want something from you, I'll ask for it!" With shambling steps, he limped to retrieve his crutch.

His dark, baleful eyes fell on Alfie. "What are *you* doing here?"

"Good morning, sir," Alfie greeted him. "I've come to help you back to your stateroom."

"Where's Tryhorn?" Masterson demanded.

Alfie struggled to be polite. "I have the honor of serving you today."

The man sighed. "Well, one dunderheaded child is as good as any other, I suppose. Come along." Leaning heavily on his crutch, he began to thump toward the door.

Alfie hurried to support his free arm, and the two stepped out into the cold air and brilliant sunlight of the boat deck.

"Is there anywhere you'd like to go this morning, sir?" Alfie inquired.

"America," Masterson replied simply. "And the sooner, the better."

Alfie forced his face into a smile. "In that case, I have good news. The captain has nearly all the boilers lit, and the *Titanic* is making superb speed. We are anticipating New York on Tuesday night, rather than Wednesday morning."

"Excellent," the man agreed. "Only when I set foot on American soil will I be free of your pointless attempts at conversation."

Smoldering with resentment, Alfie lowered his gaze. His eyes fell on a necklace he hadn't noticed before — a tiny off-white carving of a church on a leather thong.

"That's an interesting piece, sir," Alfie ventured, tight-lipped. "May I ask, is it ivory?"

"Simpleton!" Mr. Masterson quickly slipped the necklace inside the collar of his jersey. "Don't you recognize scrimshaw when you see it?"

"My father is a sailor," Alfie explained in a subdued tone. "He's brought home scrimshaw aplenty. It's a lighter shade, the color of fresh milk —"

"And your pathetic little position on this ship makes you an expert in these matters?" Masterson snapped.

Sophie waved from a nearby deck chair. "Good morning, Alfie!" She was so tightly wrapped in blankets that she resembled a mummy, a mug of hot chocolate balanced upon many layers.

As Alfie raised his arm to return the greeting, Masterson seized his wrist with astonishing strength. "I didn't ask you to serve me, but when you do, you'll not acknowledge that bird-witted American wench!"

"Miss Bronson? She's a very nice young lady!"

"Is that what you'd call the daughter of that poisonous suffragette?"

Alfie was taken aback. "I realize that not everyone supports votes for women, but —"

"It is high treason against every law of God and nature!" Mr. Masterson seethed. "There once was a time that men took action to defend the proper order of things, but no longer. We stand by while shameless women make a grab for the very essence of what makes this *our* world."

"Sir," Alfie reminded him, "you talk of our mothers and wives and sisters."

"And how, pray tell, does relation make a particle of difference? Where is the sainted mother who allows you to sell your childhood to the White Star Line?"

Until that moment, Alfie had been calm. He had tolerated Masterson's irascible manner and endured his scorn, as a steward was required to do. But to hear him speaking ill of Sarah Huggins drew a white-hot anger from deep within Alfie, from a sensitive core he didn't even know he had.

"You may heap your abuse upon me, sir," Alfie exclaimed, "but you will keep your opinions to yourself on the subject of my mother! You have not met my mother! Nor would I ever want you to!"

As he stormed down the companion stairs, the weight of what he had done descended on Alfie. He had spoken rudely to a first-class passenger. Worse, he had abandoned a lame man high up on the ship's top deck.

I'll be dismissed — as well I should be. . .

He had thrown away his chance to sail with Da — his only parent. And for what? To reproach Mr. Masterson? The man had committed grisly murders! He deserved a hangman's noose, not harsh words.

Now Captain Smith was never going to believe that Mr. Masterson was Jack the Ripper. The accusation would seem like Alfie's attempt at revenge against the passenger who had cost him his job.

Thanks to my stupidity, a horrible killer will continue to go free.

Nobody would have found that more tragic than Sarah Huggins herself. More than twenty years after the Whitechapel murders, Mum had still been obsessed with the case. Alfie had been perhaps five or six at the time, but he could still remember her exact words: *I won't sleep sound in my bed at night until that monster is off the street for good.*

He stopped in his tracks, eyes widening at the memory of Mr. Masterson's necklace. A tiny replica of a church. A white chapel — Whitechapel!

The real reason for the darker coloration of the "scrimshaw" came crashing down on him. The piece wasn't scrimshaw at all! It was another horrible souvenir of Jack the Ripper's killing spree.

The necklace was carved from human bone.

CHAPTER SEVEN

RMS *TITANIC*
SATURDAY, APRIL 13, 1912, 2:35 P.M.

The coveralls were much too large and hung on Paddy as on a small child. But as he descended the ladder to the boiler rooms, he realized that no one was likely to notice. The reddish glow from twenty-seven raging furnaces overpowered what little electric light there was. If you could keep your stinging eyes open amid the clouds of dust and steam, you were probably too distracted by the crashing, roaring din of the place to concentrate on who you saw there.

He stood, choking, at the base of the ladder, wondering if he was going to suffocate. It was like trying to breathe hot volcanic ash. How did the black gang manage it? Lungs of steel, they must have had.

Paddy had explored most of the *Titanic* since stowing away, but this was his first time in the boiler rooms. Even in Belfast, with a skeleton crew on board, this had always been a beehive of activity. Steam powered not just the enormous reciprocating engines, but also the huge dynamos that generated abundant electricity. No city in the world was as technologically advanced as the pride of the White Star Line.

He set down his water bucket, reached his hands into a coal bin, and smeared his face and neck with soot. Now he fit right in. Here, unblackened skin was a dead giveaway that you didn't belong.

Spying the bucket, a stoker dropped his shovel and strode over. Paddy handed him the dipper, and he drank thirstily.

"Thanks, lad." His voice was deep and gravelly from hard years spent in the bellies of many ships.

Paddy grunted his acknowledgment and moved on. It was risky to mingle with White Star employees. But only the dead could lie still in a closed box day and night. There were personal necessities that could not be shut off with a switch: eating, drinking, going to the water closet. And the most urgent need of all — to *do* something, *anything*, to keep from going barmy.

With the crew scouring the passenger areas for the stowaway, this was the place for Paddy — below the waterline, in the *Titanic*'s working guts.

More firemen gathered around, the dipper passed from mouth to mouth. They were tough, these stokers, even by Belfast standards. But their work was tougher still, shoveling quantities of coal that stretched to infinity, feeding a ship that was as insatiable as it was unsinkable. The members of the black gang were almost pathetically grateful for a draught of water and a small respite from their back-breaking labor.

As Paddy scanned his ash-covered customers, he was surprised to find a familiar face. The man was older, his eyes deeper-set, the soot of dozens of boiler rooms etched permanently into the lines of his skin. But the features were Alfie's.

"You're Alfie's dad!" Paddy blurted without thinking.

At the mention of his son, John Huggins softened instantly. "You know my boy?"

"He saved my life, he did," Paddy replied readily. It was a fact. Without Alfie, Paddy would have been thrown overboard by Gilhooley and Seamus.

John Huggins's pride glowed right through the layers of caked-on black. "Do tell, lad."

Paddy grew wary. The more he said, the more questions he would invite. A fugitive needed to be invisible — not the center of attention.

He hefted his bucket and banged the dipper against the side. "Water!" he barked. "Who needs a drink?"

More stokers swarmed, and Paddy was able to melt into the crowd. He worked his way aft, through the hatches that accommodated the *Titanic*'s watertight doors, and eventually found a ladder up and out.

He slumped against the bulkhead and slid down to the deck, bucket and all. What a relief to be out of that fiery place! The most luxurious ship in history, yet the biggest luxury was simply being able to breathe.

A familiar voice reached him from the far end of the passageway. "Five hundred nineteen miles! Are you certain, Joseph?"

Paddy jumped up, chagrined. In his relief at escaping the searing heat of the boiler rooms, he'd neglected to ensure that no crew members were around. He looked over to see Mr. Thomas Andrews himself, the *Titanic*'s architect, embroiled in conversation with one of the engineers.

"That was the official number, from noon Friday to Saturday," the engineer was saying. "You've built us a right racehorse, sir."

"That would make our speed" — Andrews performed the calculations in his head — "a hair better than twenty-one knots. And with two fires yet to be lit."

All at once, his eyes fell on Paddy. "Why, hello."

"Sorry to disturb you, sir." Paddy ducked his head and took a step back toward the access ladder to the boiler rooms.

"Have no fear, lad," the designer said kindly. "I'll not be reporting you for shirking your duty. I know the heat of the furnaces as well as any man. To take a wee break to cool off the burning of the skin — that's no crime."

There was a quality to Thomas Andrews that was nothing short of amazing. Here he was, the most celebrated shipbuilder in the world, a successful man with vast responsibilities. Yet he always had time for the lowliest greaser or scullery maid. Back in Belfast, he had patiently taken time to answer the questions of two ragged street urchins. He had even challenged Daniel to design a way to sink his unsinkable ship.

Through the coveralls, Paddy tapped his breast, and felt Daniel's folded drawing there. Now was the perfect opportunity to show it to the very audience it had been created for. But then Paddy would be arrested as a stowaway. Besides, what good could it possibly do for poor Daniel, who was already dead?

Mr. Andrews peered at Paddy in sudden interest. "Have we met before?"

Paddy hurriedly lowered his eyes. "Engine crew, sir." He held up the bucket. "I bring water to the men."

The designer nodded, frowning. "Funny, I thought I knew you from somewhere else." And he and the engineer disappeared around the corner on the way to other urgent business.

CHAPTER EIGHT

Alfie was well acquainted with the baggage hold. In the many hours he had spent there, searching for the source of the Jack the Ripper scrapbook, he had learned the locations of most of his passengers' luggage. It was the work of but a few moments to find the Bronson trunk and open it with the shiny metal key Mrs. Bronson had provided.

He lifted the lid. There was surprisingly little clothing for two first-class ladies. Instead, the majority of the space was taken up with large bundles of printed pamphlets, brochures, and posters blazoning the slogans of the suffrage cause. VOTES FOR WOMEN NOW! declared one. Another proclaimed: 2ND CLASS CITIZENS NO LONGER! There were also handbills advertising rallies all across England featuring Amelia Bronson. No wonder Sophie's mother had crossed the ocean just to make a few speeches. She was her move-ment's shining beacon.

He removed an armload of literature and locked the trunk again. That was Alfie's errand in the hold — to fetch a selection for Mrs. Bronson. Before return-ing to the upper decks, he slipped under the netting that secured the Astors' luggage. "Paddy, are you awake?" he whispered. "I've brought you some bread."

He eased open the lid of the linen trunk and peered inside. The outline of Paddy's compact frame was evi-dent in the fine fabric. The stowaway himself was nowhere in sight.

It was not a great shock — no one could be expected to spend days on end lying in a steamer trunk. But it was worrisome just the same — for Paddy's sake and also for Alfie's. If the stowaway were to be caught, Mr. Lightoller's first question would likely be, "Who has been helping you?"

Alfie found Mrs. Bronson on the enclosed prome-nade on B Deck, seventy vertical feet above her luggage. There she stood, resplendent in purple, white, and green, in the company of her daughter and Juliana.

"The pamphlets you wanted, ma'am," he panted, out of breath from the climb.

"Thank you, Alfie. I'm sure the major will find these very enlightening."

"The *major*?" Sophie was amazed. "These are for Major Muttonchop?"

Her mother nodded. "He specifically asked for them."

"You're fooling yourself. His interest in suffrage is nothing more than a ploy to ensnare you to listen to his war stories, his hunting stories, his school stories, and everything else that's happened to him since he graduated from the cradle."

"I'd like to read one," Juliana ventured timidly.

Mrs. Bronson beamed at the prospect of a new recruit. "May you never know the humiliation that your mother and grandmother continue to endure," she said, handing over a selection of leaflets.

"If I were you," Sophie offered, "I wouldn't show those to your father. His lordship doesn't strike me as the suffrage type."

"In that case, *definitely* show them to your father," her mother countered. "You cannot expect real change unless you're willing to shake things up a bit."

Sophie sniffed. "Is that why you spend so many of your nights in prison cells?"

The suffragist was untroubled. "A prison cell is far more agreeable to me than the ridiculous, unnecessary comforts of this ship — if it means I'm getting attention for the cause."

"The one in London had rats," her daughter reminded her with a shudder.

"There are worse things than rats, Sophie. Pig-headed men who are keeping half the population as second-class citizens come to mind."

"Excuse me." Junior Steward Tryhorn approached the group and took Alfie aside. "He wants you," he said in a low voice.

Alfie smiled apologetically at the three ladies and turned his attention to the newcomer. "He? Who?"

"Masterson. He asked for you by name."

Alfie's heart sank into his boots. This was it, then. If Mr. Masterson had sent for him, the purpose was surely to denounce him to one of the officers. His future as a White Star Line employee — and Da's crewmate — was over.

"Where is he?" Alfie asked finally. "Was there anyone with him? Mr. Lightoller, perhaps?"

"He's in his stateroom," Tryhorn replied. "He rang for a steward, and when I arrived, he was his usual charming self. He threw me out and demanded you. The old rotter!"

"You're the lucky one," Alfie groaned. "I have to deal with the man."

The irony of it was enough to make him weep. He was about to be condemned and ruined *by Jack the Ripper*!

He sighed. "All right, I'll go. But if you don't hear from me, send out a search party." He faced Mrs. Bronson, her daughter, and Juliana once more. "If you'll excuse me, ladies, Mr. Masterson requires my attention."

"Take along a chair and a whip," Mrs. Bronson advised darkly. "That's a nasty piece of work if ever I met one."

Sophie was shocked. "Mother! What an unkind thing to say!"

"It's not unkind if it's the truth. I see the way that man looks at me — at all women. He hates us."

"I admit that he's not the nicest person aboard," Sophie conceded. "But it can't be easy to be him. He's probably in pain every time he tries to walk."

"I understand suffering," Amelia Bronson replied. "Woman-hatred is a separate matter. It is the product of a sick mind. Don't turn your back on him, Alfie dear."

As he trudged up the companion stairs to A Deck, Alfie wondered how seriously he should take Mrs.

Bronson's warning. She certainly had an instinct for the evil that emanated from Mr. Masterson. After all, Jack the Ripper was the most notorious woman-hater of all time.

And now he has every reason to be angry with me. . . .

Of course, the man was old and crippled now. But his upper-body strength was nothing short of miraculous. Alfie would do well to stay alert behind the closed door of stateroom A-17.

That door appeared before him, and he knocked lightly.

"Enter," came a gruff voice. "What took you so long? You had a more pressing engagement?"

Alfie stepped inside, making sure to leave the stateroom door open. "How may I help you, sir?"

Masterson sat in an overstuffed armchair, his crutch close at hand. He looked up defiantly. "I require your assistance to get on with my day."

The wave of relief nearly knocked Alfie flat. For some reason, this disagreeable old beast did not intend to turn him in for his rudeness earlier on. There was only one thing that didn't make sense.

"Steward Tryhorn is assigned to you, sir. He is more than capable of seeing to your needs."

"That ninnyhammer?" the old man scoffed. "He can barely see to his own needs. I want you."

Alfie swallowed hard. "I had the impression that you found my service unsatisfactory."

"You're not paid to form impressions," Masterson growled. "Still, you're the only person on this gilded barge with any backbone. I like that."

Alfie shut his eyes for a brief dizzy moment. To be liked by Jack the Ripper! Oh, what would Mum say?

"Thank you, sir. I'm happy to be able to be of assistance."

The old man laughed. "No, you're not. You'd like to take my crutch and beat me over the head with it. Admit it. You think I don't know I'm a cantankerous old louse? You try dragging yourself around on two gammy legs and see how sunny your disposition is."

Alfie began tidying the nightstand, straightening pill bottles and laying out fresh handkerchiefs. It helped not to be looking at Masterson directly. It was hard to carry on a conversation while gazing into those hooded cobra eyes.

"Might I ask you, sir," Alfie ventured, "how long you've had this regrettable condition? Have you always been thus?"

"No, not always, more's the pity. Many years ago,

I was a strapping young lad going about my business. I don't even remember what spooked that horse — some say lightning. The passengers in the carriage were both killed. They were the lucky ones. I was crushed under the wheels. Spinal damage."

"*You* were the lucky one," Alfie said seriously. "You have your life."

"You call this a life, boy?" Masterson spat. "Twenty-four years ago, I was doing important work! Accomplishing something! Without it, I'm less than a man."

Important work! The words chilled Alfie to his core. Could Jack the Ripper have looked upon his killing spree as a mission? If it hadn't been for that carriage accident, the grisly Whitechapel murders might have continued!

"I'm very sorry, sir," he managed at last. "But you do have your visit to America to look forward to. That should be pleasant."

"This is no pleasure trip, boy," Masterson barked. "I've been in correspondence with a doctor in New York who thinks he can cure me!"

Silent horror whispered over Alfie. "Cure you?" he echoed faintly.

"I have hopes," Masterson admitted. "Of course, I am no longer young. But to be *me* again, to be free of this prison of my own body! If America could give me this gift, there is nothing I would not offer in return!"

Alfie's mind raced. What would it mean if Mr. Masterson were to be cured and suddenly turned loose upon the city of New York? Would he resume the "important work" that had ceased twenty-four years ago because of his accident? Would America begin to have its own Whitechapel murders?

"In fact," the old man went on, "I have a message for my American doctor for you to take to the Marconi room." He handed Alfie a folded note. "See that this is sent immediately."

As Alfie ascended into the brilliant sunshine of the boat deck, he cradled the paper in his trembling hands as if it were an explosive device.

A message from Jack the Ripper!

Barely daring to breathe, he opened the page and peered at the contents.

Arriving Titanic *Wednesday. Expect office visit Thursday, poss. Friday. Masterson*

Alfie was almost disappointed. It was just a man confirming an appointment.

Still, he couldn't escape the feeling that, by sending the Marconigram, he would be aiding in the rebirth of the dreaded Whitechapel murderer.

Yet he had no choice but to do it. Mr. Masterson would expect to see the receipt from the Marconi company.

Oh, Mum, if you only knew what your son has gotten himself into!

Aboard the *Titanic*, even the wireless room looked luxurious, with dark paneling and thick, elegant carpets. Although the tables were cluttered with transmitters and receivers, they were ornate French pieces of the highest quality.

Normally, only one operator at a time manned the equipment. But today, both Jack Phillips and Harold Bride were busy sending messages, their fingers working furiously, tapping out Morse code. Neither noticed Alfie in the doorway.

He cleared his throat. "I have a Marconigram from Mr. Masterson in A-17."

"It'll have to wait," said Phillips without looking up.

Alfie shuffled uncomfortably. "Mr. Masterson is not the sort of gentleman who waits patiently. Or quietly."

Bride indicated an enormous stack of messages skewered on a metal spike marked *outgoing*. "Every well-heeled toff aboard this ship wants to make sure his well-heeled friends and business associates know that he's on the maiden voyage of the *Titanic*. When the Astors and the Guggenheims and the Strauses and all the others have had their expensive say, your Mr. Masterson will have the privilege of spending too much money to communicate very little to someone very far away."

Tight-lipped, Alfie impaled his message on the spike. Mr. Masterson wouldn't like this. "Will you deliver the receipt?"

"Oh, certainly!" snorted Bride. "We've got loads of time for that. That's the part where I stick a mop handle up my trousers so I can swab the deck while I'm running!"

"Don't mind him," Phillips said. "He doesn't like being overworked unto death." He held out a handwritten sheet to Alfie. "Listen, old man, will you take this message to the bridge for me? All ice warnings have to go to the captain directly."

Alfie read the time notation. "This is from three hours ago!"

"Well, this one's fresh," put in Bride, handing over another sheet.

Alfie scanned it. "How much ice is out there?"

Phillips shrugged. "Could be the same berg being reported by two different ships. Don't get your knickers in a twist. April's the time for ice. The Arctic gets warmer, the glaciers calve — it happens every year."

There was a sudden series of pops. Sparks flew, electricity sizzled. A billow of smoke engulfed the equipment.

Bride cursed. "Not again!"

His partner waved a sheaf of Marconi forms in an effort to clear away the cloud.

"I hope you weren't planning on sleeping tonight," Phillips groaned. "It's going to take hours to put this back together." He turned to Alfie. "Go! And tell them the wireless is down again."

Alfie took the short walk forward to the bridge.

Fourth Officer Boxhall was at the wheel. Also present were Mr. Lightoller, Captain Smith, and J. Bruce Ismay, the managing director of the White Star Line.

Lightoller noticed the young steward first. "And you are —?"

"Alphonse Huggins, sir."

The second officer's heavy eyebrows rose. "Huggins, is it? So you're the one the stowaway mentioned. How might you explain that he knew your name?"

"Maybe he saw it on a crew manifest," Alfie suggested timidly.

Lightoller grunted. "And what's your business on the bridge, Huggins?"

"Trouble in the Marconi room," Alfie reported. "Mr. Phillips said it will take several hours to repair."

The second officer emitted a short mirthless laugh. "If men were meant to communicate across oceans, the good Lord would have given us louder voices."

"And there are two ice warnings for the captain," Alfie added, taking out the papers.

"I'll take those," Lightoller said.

Alfie held them away. "I believe the protocol is that they must be placed directly in the captain's hands, sir."

Amused, Lightoller stepped aside, and Alfie approached the commodore of the line.

"I know the speed has been impressive," Mr. Ismay was saying as Alfie drew near, "but you know she can do better."

Captain Smith took the messages from Alfie, glanced at them briefly, and turned back to Ismay. "Yes, but *should* she do better?"

"Well, of course she should!" Ismay exclaimed. "Don't you want to see what she can do with those last two furnaces fired up? Naturally, I'm just a passenger, but I certainly do."

Captain Smith seemed to chew this over for a moment. Then he called to his second officer: "Mr. Lightoller, order the last two boilers lit. By all means, let's see what she can do."

Alfie looked on in confusion. The two ice warnings were still in the captain's hands.

CHAPTER NINE

RMS *TITANIC*
Saturday, April 13, 1912, 9:05 p.m.

Still clad in the baggy coveralls, Paddy climbed to the top of the aft third-class staircase. In his hand he clutched a bouquet of exquisite white orchids.

Sixteen-year-old Curran Rankin laughed at the sight of him. "Well, would you look at this? If it isn't my onetime brother Patrick! Are you getting married with those flowers, Paddy?"

"They're for your ma," Paddy grinned, "fresh from the first-class dining saloon. If it's good enough for millionaires, it's good enough for the sweetest lady who ever hid a fellow from a nosy sailor."

"Aw, she was glad to do it. What's one boy more or less when she's already got so many?"

"Where is she now? In the cabin?"

"Follow me." Curran led him through the passageways of third class, past the Rankins' cabin, moving steadily aft.

"Where are we going?" Paddy wondered, noting that there were a lot of passengers in the corridors, all heading in the same direction. "Don't tell me steerage has to ride on the propellers now."

Curran laughed. "Shhh. Don't give the White Star Line any ideas. This way. I promise you'll not be sorry."

They bustled up a crowded staircase and entered the third-class general room. That was where Paddy first heard the music — a tin whistle and a fiddle playing an upbeat Irish jig.

By now the migration was more like a stampede, rushing across the room in an effort to reach . . . what?

At last, Paddy burst into the open air of the aft well deck and into the heart of the largest party he'd ever seen. Hundreds of steerage passengers danced and stomped and clapped along with the music.

Curran beamed at him. "We may not have their fancy champagne and waiters in monkey suits. But when it comes to having a good time, we could show those swells a thing or two."

Paddy held his bouquet high in the air to keep it from being crushed. Although the night was frigid, the heat generated by so many moving bodies kept the temperature comfortable.

And the music! Not even in Belfast had he heard its like. It was the heartbeat of hundreds of tiny villages throughout Ireland, like his own in County Antrim. It was the sound of home.

A hand grabbed his shoulder and spun him around. He knew a moment of panic.

How will I flee in this huge crowd?

"Don't look so pale, darlin' — it's only me!" Mrs. Rankin pulled him into a loving hug, thoroughly squashing the flowers between them. "Were those for me? Aren't you sweet!" She held up the stems. "I'm sure they were lovely!"

Paddy had to shout to be heard over the music and the noise of the crowd. "I wanted to thank you and make sure you didn't get into any trouble because of me."

"Everything's fine, Paddy," she assured him. "Come on — dance with your ma."

Paddy shrank back. "I shouldn't. The officers know I've been hiding in third class."

"Do you really think we'd let any stuffed-shirt English take one of our own?" she demanded. "Now I'll have that dance."

Paddy gave in gracefully. His toes were beginning to tap, anyway.

☆

"We're coming, Alfie!"

Juliana struggled to keep pace with the young steward, who was towing both girls aft along the boat deck. "You don't have to wrench our arms out of their sockets!"

Alfie did not let go of their hands. "I don't want you to miss this," he exclaimed, urging them to greater speed.

"Miss what?" Sophie puffed. "What's so wonderful that we have to choke down our dessert and make an Olympic dash the length of the ship?"

"Humor me," Alfie pleaded. "After an entire day at the beck and call of a tyrant like Mr. Masterson, I need something to make me smile. And some friends to share it with."

"I would expect you to have a little more sympathy for a poor cripple," Sophie told him disapprovingly.

Alfie's face darkened. "Save your sympathy for someone who deserves it."

They passed beneath the fourth funnel and descended the companion stairs to the second-class promenade.

A small crowd had gathered at the rail, but Juliana could not make out what they were watching. Spirited music played below, and she could hear the hubbub of many excited voices as well as the rhythm of stomping feet.

At last, Alfie wormed his way to the overlook, drawing the girls with him. Beneath them, the aft well deck teemed with humanity — hundreds of passengers dancing and singing and celebrating. The crowd was so dense that not an inch of planking was visible. It was a blizzard of color and motion, all set to a sprightly beat.

To say it was lively was an understatement. It was life. And if the clothes were more drab and less elegant than the fine fabrics and glittering jewels found in first class, the revelers made up for it with energy and enthusiasm.

"I'm jealous," Sophie murmured in awe. "First class paid all the money, and steerage is having all the fun."

Alfie beamed. "I knew you'd want to see it."

Juliana was bewildered. She had only observed members of the lower classes performing a function — storekeeper, chambermaid, hackney driver. She had never considered that Mrs. Musgrave, their housekeeper, had a life of her own apart from her duties to the Glamm family. Yet here were people precisely like that — hundreds of them — not performing any function at all. They were just enjoying themselves.

Her eyes found one particularly agile dancer. Even though he was clad in heavy, soot-stained coveralls, his arms and legs moved with athletic grace and something close to joy.

The other dancers noticed him, too, and stopped to watch, forming an ever-widening circle around him. The extra space lent wings to his feet, and he whirled like a top to the fiddler's tune. His features were just a blur until the spin slowed, and . . .

Sophie leaned forward, frowning. "Wait. Isn't that —?"

"Paddy!" Alfie rasped, horrified.

"Why is he in the middle of that party?" Juliana mused. "He doesn't know those people."

"He's a very talented dancer," Sophie commented, impressed.

"I don't care if he's the King of Siam!" Alfie exclaimed. "He's supposed to be in hiding! Why is he waving himself in front of the entire ship? Has he gone daft?"

"He was always daft," Sophie pointed out. "This is just the latest part of it."

Juliana turned to the young steward. "You have to do something about this, Alfie! I didn't risk my reputation lying to protect him just to watch him hand himself over to the officers!"

By the end of her speech, she was talking to empty air. Alfie was already sprinting for the superstructure and the nearest staircase.

"Bless my soul!" came an all-too-familiar voice behind them. Major Mountjoy's stomach pushed its way to the rail. "I asked myself: Mountjoy, what is the big attraction on the second-class promenade? But now that I see you two beautiful ladies here, my question has answered itself."

Juliana and Sophie exchanged an agonized glance. There were times when both girls were willing to be polite and humor Major Muttonchop. But this was not one of those times.

They ran off after Alfie.

"My word, where are you going?" the major called in dismay.

"Down there!" Sophie tossed over her shoulder.

Amazed, Major Mountjoy peered over the rail at the revelry in the well deck. "But — but — that's *steerage* class!"

The girls entered the superstructure just as Alfie disappeared down the steps. They followed at a heart-pounding pace, exiting where the music seemed the loudest. They ran out onto the well deck to be stopped by a solid wall of bodies.

"Excuse me," Juliana said formally.

No one heard her, not even Sophie, who was right beside her. Sophie grabbed her friend by the elbow and plowed her way through the crowd.

Never before had the daughter of the Earl of Glamford been subjected to such an experience — to be squeezed through a mass of people like frosting out the narrow opening of a cake decorator bag. It was Sophie who seemed to know exactly what to do in such painfully close quarters, probably from experience at her mother's suffrage rallies. She moved with confidence, while it was all Juliana could do to keep from fainting.

She could feel eyes upon them, some curious, some hostile. Their fine silks and velvets gave them away as anything but third class.

When they finally pushed to the center of the throng, an appalling sight greeted them. A huge strapping Irish boy had Alfie in a headlock, and several others stood by, fists balled, poses menacing.

"He's not arresting me!" Paddy was shouting over the din. "It's all right! He's my friend!" He saw the girls standing in front of him. "What are you two doing here?"

All Juliana's uneasiness was turned instantly to anger by that question.

"What are *we* doing here? What are *you* doing here? We've all risked our necks to protect you! And how do you repay us? You just about write your name on a banner and fly it across the smokestacks! Are you actually insane, or merely stupid?"

Curran Rankin was highly amused. "Paddy, I never knew your mother was a rich English lady. How come you turned out so poor and ugly?"

Paddy faced the two girls. "I'm safe here. Look around you. I've got an army! They were ready to throw Alfie in the drink just for wearing a White Star uniform!"

"And how long will your army last if the officers come with pistols?" Sophie challenged.

"I'll hide," Paddy promised. "Later. But for now I just want to have a little fun."

At those words, the fiddler started up again. Paddy grabbed each of the girls by the hand. "Come on, now. When are two fancy ladies going to have the chance to dance with a desperate character who's two steps ahead of the coppers?"

Before they knew it, Paddy was teaching them the Irish jig. Sophie had natural rhythm, and took to it immediately. But Juliana felt her years of dance lessons holding her back. The formal steps she'd been taught since she'd first learned to walk were not serving her here.

Paddy read her mind. "There's no wrong way to do it!" he shouted over the commotion. "Just let go!"

Juliana wondered if that was even possible for the daughter of the seventeenth Earl of Glamford.

CHAPTER TEN

RMS *TITANIC*
SATURDAY, APRIL 13, 1912, 10:10 P.M.

Too much gaming.

According to Elizabeth, Countess of Glamford, that was her husband's biggest weakness.

The earl knew this to be untrue. The problem was not too much gaming. It was too much losing.

Weaving slightly, he stepped out of the first-class lounge and made his way to the boat deck for some air. If he could clear his head, perhaps he could go back for a few more hands. Maybe his luck was about to change. . . .

Belay that. Mountjoy was coming toward him, probably armed with a few million well-chosen words. If the earl allowed himself to be drawn into one of the man's interminable stories, he'd never make it back to the lounge.

He turned into the shadow of a tall ventilation

outlet and pretended to be lighting a cigarette. The ruse failed.

"Ahoy, Glamford," the major called jovially. "A pleasant good evening to you."

"Mountjoy," the earl barely acknowledged.

"I must congratulate you, sir. You and the countess have raised a remarkable young lady. Her ability to interact with all classes of society does her — and you — great credit."

The earl's eyes grew watchful. "My daughter? Juliana?"

"At this very moment, she is in the aft well deck at a dance party."

"Mountjoy, what are you saying?" the earl exclaimed. "Nobody goes to the aft well deck! It's in steerage!"

"Exactly." The major smiled. "*All* classes of society, including that one. Good night, your lordship. Sleep well."

No one had ever seen Rodney, Earl of Glamford move so fast. He rushed down the companion stairs to the second-class promenade. The spectators were lined up three deep at the rail, and he had to peer over heads to see the well deck below.

The revelry and abandon was most distasteful. But what did one expect of the steerage?

And then his eyes, panning the raucous scene, found his daughter.

She was dancing. No, that term was far too civilized to describe it. She was a frenzy of movement, her head thrown back, her hair coming down loose and flying. The expression on her face was pure enjoyment — one might even call it bliss.

For a young woman of her birth and station, it was completely unacceptable.

The American was with her — Sophie — equally misbehaving, although that mother of hers would probably find this socially progressive. Both Juliana and Sophie were hanging off the arms of a boy in dirty work attire. And at close quarters all around them — touching, even — were these *persons*! Emigrants! Foreigners! And who knew what else!

Words failed him. How could the White Star Line permit such a thing? Aboard the premier ocean liner on the face of the earth, a gentleman should not have to worry about protecting his daughter's reputation!

He stormed back up to the boat deck and collared the first White Star uniform he encountered.

"What kind of ship are you running here? Steerage is in full chaos and riot, and young girls are being lured to take part in immoral dancing and revelry!"

The poor assistant pantryman had only come for

some air before going to bed. The last thing he'd expected was to be set upon by an irate nobleman. He stood there, speechless, his ears blistered, as the earl raged on.

"May I be of some assistance, your lordship?" came a quiet voice at his elbow.

The earl wheeled and found himself face-to-face with Second Officer Charles Herbert Lightoller.

"Yes, you may! There is a scene of anarchy and debauchery taking place in the aft well deck!"

Lightoller smiled deferentially. "The steerage passengers have few comforts, and very little to entertain them. We try not to begrudge them their little parties, however vulgar they may appear to us."

"Little parties?" the earl exploded. "I'll have you know that my young daughter has been practically kidnapped and forced to take part!"

The second officer's face grew grim. "Understood. I shall return her to your stateroom at once."

He descended to the second-class overlook and peered down at the whirling dancers. He found Sophie and Juliana almost immediately. Their colorful evening wear made them two lilies in a hayfield.

Pity, he thought briefly, to interrupt their youthful fun. But if the earl said it was inappropriate, why, so it was.

His eyes fell on the two girls' dance partner — the slight figure in coveralls whose swift movements made his features just a blur.

The song ended; the dancers stopped. And the boy's face finally came into focus.

Lightoller bristled. It was the stowaway.

CHAPTER ELEVEN

RMS *TITANIC*
SATURDAY, APRIL 13, 1912, 10:25 P.M.

Paddy Burns was remembering what it was like to be happy.

It was the speed that made it work, he decided. As if his constant motion could unwind all the bad luck that had befallen him — the poverty of his family, the brutality of his stepfather, the squalor of his street life in Belfast, the murder of his best friend by the Gilhooleys, and his life as a hunted animal aboard the *Titanic*. None of it could touch him as long as he kept moving.

He danced on winged feet, twirling the girls as the steerage passengers thronged around, stamping their boots and clapping. Even Alfie, whose face was pinched and anxious, was bobbing his head in time with the music.

The stomping rhythm broke first. The crowd began to struggle and then part. Second Officer Lightoller bulled through the dancers, flanked by two able seamen.

Sophie spotted them first. "Paddy — *run*!"

Before Paddy could react, Lightoller's fist locked onto his wrist. Struggle though he might, Paddy could not break the steel grip.

Juliana did the only thing she could think of. With a cry of "I feel faint!" she threw herself forward, trusting the second officer's chivalry.

He did not fail her. He released Paddy and caught her sagging form just before she hit the deck. When he looked back again, Paddy was gone.

After that, the chaos was complete. The revelers stood back to open an escape route for Paddy, but closed ranks for the second officer and his men, blocking them at every turn. No one physically interfered with them, but the third-class passengers would not make way, no matter how loudly Lightoller bellowed.

Paddy scrambled out of the well deck via a steep companionway and looked around. From the rail, a heavy line stretched overhead — one of the guy wires anchoring the after mast. Breathing a silent prayer, he shinnied up the taut rope and dropped down to the second-class promenade, well behind the spectators watching the party below.

He dashed around the corner, leaped the gate, and slipped into the side entrance of the Verandah Café.

It was one of the most stunning rooms on the ship, featuring ivy-covered black lattice on the walls and immaculate white wicker furniture. The café was deserted except for a lone server collecting dirty dishes. He stared at the newcomer in dirty coveralls. "You can't be in here!"

"They sent me to help clean up," Paddy panted.

"What? Dressed like that?"

Paddy heard footsteps outside the door and knew he had no time to argue with the waiter. "I'm supposed to *help*!" He grabbed the tray from the bewildered man, tipped it up, and flipped the contents toward the door.

His timing could not have been more perfect. As Lightoller entered, he was pelted with drinks, cold coffee, and half-finished desserts. Glassware and ashtrays shattered at his feet.

Paddy bolted out of the café, leaving a trail of overturned tables in his wake. It wouldn't slow down the second officer much, but he hoped it would give him enough of a cushion to disappear.

He sprinted along the passageway, looking left and right for a ladder or stair — anything that would get him off A Deck. There it was — a steep stewards' ramp. He ran for it, disappearing just as Lightoller burst from the café.

Seeing no sign of his quarry, the second officer reached for the communication telephone on the bulkhead.

Paddy's ramp bypassed B Deck and went directly to C. As he ran down the passageway, he kicked out of his coveralls and left them on the carpet behind him. Let them think he was on C. Let them search every compartment and storeroom. That ought to keep them busy for a while. He would be nowhere near here.

He took the stairs to E Deck and wheeled onto Scotland Road. Following this route, he could be all the way forward in the bow of the ship in minutes, far from Lightoller's last sighting of him.

He slowed down to a brisk walk. Scotland Road wasn't as busy now as it was during the day. But there were certainly crew about, and too much obvious haste would attract their attention. He received a few curious glances, and wondered whether scuttling the coveralls might have been a mistake. He was in the shirt and breeches of a third-class boy again, and that wasn't the best costume for the working parts of the ship.

But he never made it to the bow, or anywhere near

it. After perhaps fifty yards, he spied a sailor talking on one of the bulkhead telephones. More important, that sailor spied him.

If the thought had occurred to him a few seconds later, he probably would have been caught.

He's speaking to the bridge! They've got a ship-wide alert for me!

He fled, leaping the rail of an access ladder and climbing down out of view. As he descended, the very ship around him seemed to fade out. He was suspended in darkness, clinging to the rungs in what seemed to be an endless vertical passage.

Noises swelled — a mechanical *thrum* punctuated by a vibration he could feel in his gut. Now he knew what lay below him. He had found the way down to the ship's vast reciprocating engines.

As his eyes adjusted to the low light, he could make out a system of heavy piping, which brought in the steam that turned huge armatures. They looked otherworldly and alive, like the arms of giants performing a never-ending ritual.

At last he saw the deck, and stepped off onto something solid. With a sinking heart, Paddy spotted the engineer and recognized the device at his ear — a telephone receiver. Even here, in the bowels of the ship, Lightoller had found him.

In growing panic, Paddy understood that the game had changed. He was quick enough and smart enough to avoid a single officer aboard this floating city. But thanks to the *Titanic*'s communication phones, he was now the prey of more than nine hundred crew members, not just one.

With his heart thumping in his chest, he ran straight into the heart of all that massive machinery, hoping to disappear amid the forest of supports that held the engine in place. Over his shoulder, he caught sight of a mammoth armature plunging toward him.

In a blind panic, he flung himself to the deck. He closed his eyes, waiting to be squashed like a bug by tons of steel.

CHAPTER TWELVE

RMS *TITANIC*
SATURDAY, APRIL 13, 1912, 10:35 P.M.

The huge mechanical appendage swung down through the bottom of its range of motion, passing inches above Paddy's cowering form.

"Come on out, lad," the engineer called. "You can't hide forever."

Paddy raised his head slightly, casting his eyes over his surroundings. Had he well and truly trapped himself here? The *Titanic* was so vast and interconnected that there was almost always another path. . . .

He spotted it between two support pillars — a small hatch in the forward bulkhead. Even if it led straight out the side of the hull into the ocean, he had already decided to go there. He peered up at the armatures, timing their motion. The instant the head space was clear, he was sprinting for the opening.

"Stop!" the engineer cried.

But before the man could translate his words into

action, Paddy was through the hatch. The blast of heat nearly knocked him backward.

The furnaces! I'm in Number 1 Boiler Room!

Spitting ash, he scampered past a coal bunker, risking a glance to the rear. The engineer stumbled after him, bellowing at top volume. Paddy could distinctly make out the word "stowaway."

Now the fat's in the fire.

He fairly flung himself at the access ladder, scrambling like a monkey. Within seconds, he could feel the vibration of pursuers below him. A reaching hand grabbed his boot, and he kicked frantically, making contact with something solid. A muffled cry of pain, and he was free again. He scrambled up on deck and looked around wildly. He was on F now — just aft of the third-class dining saloon.

Running along the passage, he glanced over his shoulder and counted four crewmen chasing him — the angry engineer followed by three stokers. The scene reminded Paddy of a child's storybook Daniel had shown him about an English fox hunt. At the time, Paddy had felt sorry for the fox.

Now I am the fox!

He dashed into the darkened third-class galley, searching for a place to hide. There were nooks and crannies aplenty, but nowhere that he wouldn't be discovered by someone who was looking hard enough.

The indecision cost him precious seconds. The door swung open, slapping against the bulkhead. Bright light from the corridor penetrated the kitchen. There was no time to flee. In another instant, the crewmen would be upon him.

Acting on pure mindless instinct, Paddy rammed his shoulder into a stack of crates. Falling boxes hit the deck, sending the engineer sprawling. The wooden sides splintered apart, and, all at once, eleven large cantaloupes were rolling across the deck like a wave. A stoker's boot came down on a spinning melon. With a cry of dismay, the man went down, bowling out the two pursuers behind him.

Paddy pounded through the third-class dining saloon, vaulting over long communal tables and benches. Back in the passageways, he felt the difference right down to the tips of his toes — the soft, thick carpeting of a first-class corridor. Some of the *Titanic*'s most luxurious features were on this part of F Deck — the heated saltwater swimming pool and the legendary Turkish steam bath.

Neither held the slightest interest for Paddy now. Escape was his singular thought.

He knew where he was heading without consciously deciding to go there — as if his legs were under the control of a puppeteer. It was the one hiding place aboard ship he'd hoped he'd never have to use — a place so cold, so dark, so dreadful that it made the hair stand up on the back of his neck just to think about it. Only if there was no other choice, he'd told himself when he'd first discovered it.

At a full gallop, he reentered the working part of the ship, jogging left and right as he made his way toward the prow. He could feel the bulkheads closing in as the hull tapered. He raced through the firemen's quarters, past sleeping stokers, trying his best to skim silently across the deck.

When he saw the hatch, he pulled up short, almost choking on the lump that suddenly rose in his throat.

The pounding feet in the distance made the decision for him. It was either the misery that lay beyond this hatch, or the brig with the murderous Gilhooleys. No contest.

He threw open the heavy door to be greeted by a blast of frigid air and the overpowering smell of lubricant. And there it was, the *Titanic*'s anchor chain, a vast pile of enormous black links, each of them nearly Paddy's full height.

He stepped out onto the curved, stout iron, finding it slick with grease. This was even more dangerous than he'd originally feared. He looked down. There was nothing to see but chain, folded in upon itself, all the way to the bilge of the ship, some forty feet below. Above him, the chain disappeared into the narrow shaft that stretched all the way to where the anchor hung on the starboard side of the prow.

He straddled the link and wrapped his arm around another. Only then did he feel secure enough to reach out and pull the hatch shut behind him. The darkness was almost smothering, enveloping him like a black velvet curtain. He unhitched his suspenders and tied them around the heavy iron, hoping against hope that they would support his weight in case he slipped. He seriously doubted that they would. If he dozed and lost his purchase on the link, he would be bruised, bloody, and dashed to pieces in the bilge. By the time his body was discovered there, if indeed it ever was, he would be nothing but a pitiful pile of broken bones.

Time passed with such agonizing slowness that minutes seemed like months. Paddy had no way of clocking his ordeal, yet he knew one thing for certain: He had to stay in the chain locker as long as was humanly possible. Second Officer Lightoller was not the sort of man who gave up easily. This search was going to take all night.

He shuddered, which made the grease run up his arms and down his legs. Paddy Burns had survived much in his fourteen years.

He was not at all certain he was going to survive this.

CHAPTER THIRTEEN

It wasn't sleep, exactly, but rather a frozen stupor brought on by exhaustion, bone-chilling cold, and the cramping of every muscle in his body in the effort to maintain his perch on the greasy anchor chain. The terror of falling had now become so old that he was losing his sharpness — even dozing a little. And disaster could be the only result of that.

How long had he been in this otherworldly place? It was impossible to tell. Long enough to lose feeling in his arms and legs. If he ever got out of here — if he ever opened that hatch and returned to the land of the living, he was by no means sure that his body would support him.

The hatch!

It was then that he realized that he was looking at the hatch. Its edges were lined with faint light. That meant daylight, morning.

I've survived the night!

For all the horror he'd already endured, this next move was surely the riskiest. He was about to open the hatch and quite possibly step into the arms of some stoker, who would deliver him directly to Mr. Lightoller's swift justice.

But it had to be done. Five more minutes here and he might never recover enough to save himself. He undid the suspenders that were holding him in place. They fell and he never heard them land. Then he reached over, unlocked the hatch, and swung the door wide. An instant later, with more pain than he'd ever dreamed imaginable, he was standing on the deck, trembling and faint with fatigue.

But he was alone! By sheer luck, he had managed to find a moment in which all the firemen were gone from their quarters — a shift change, perhaps.

He took a step toward the door and froze. Slimy lubricating grease dripped from him with every movement. A quick self-inspection revealed that he was covered with the stuff from head to foot.

The urge to run — to get out of here before the stokers returned — was almost overwhelming. He fought it down. Begrimed with sludge, he'd leave a trail of black wherever he went.

He stripped off his filthy clothes and stepped into the adjoining shower room. The water was nearly scalding, yet the heat brought life to his numb fingers and toes, and eased the stiffness in his muscles. It was lucky that firemen used strong, gritty soap to combat the boilers' ash, because the muck on his skin did not remove easily. After much scrubbing, he turned off the spray, feeling strangely awake and alive. For Paddy, a wash usually meant a swim in an ice-cold lake or river. Hot water and real soap was quite a luxury.

He pulled on a pair of coveralls hanging on a hook, rolling up the cuffs several times at the wrists and ankles. Kicking on his boots, he strode out of the shower room — and very nearly collided with the stoker standing by one of the bunks.

Paddy cast his gaze down to the deck. "Morning," he mumbled in the deepest voice he could muster.

"How do you know my son?" the man demanded. "How do you know Alfie?"

Oh, Lord, Alfie's father!

Paddy toyed with trusting in his natural gift of blarney and trying to talk his way out of this. But more crewmen could be coming any minute — and surely some of them knew about last night's manhunt.

Perhaps Mr. Huggins himself did. There was suspicion in his gruff voice. . . .

With a cry of "I'm late!" Paddy dove for an access ladder and began a hurried descent, made agonizing by the aching of his arms and legs. He had no idea where he was going — possibly down to the hostile territory of the boiler rooms.

No. Cargo surrounded him, lashed to angled bulkheads. He was in the forward hold, just aft of the bow's peak.

That means it isn't far to the baggage room!

He dashed through the fireman's passage and burst through the familiar hatch.

His exhaustion mingled with a surge of triumph. He'd been on the run for eight hours, but he'd made it.

He slipped under the netting and crawled into the large steamer trunk that was the closest thing to a safe place he would ever know aboard the *Titanic.* Curled up on Mrs. Astor's fine linens, he fell into the deepest sleep he could remember.

☆

When Alfie was shaken awake in his bunk, he very nearly swallowed his heart.

Lightoller! He saw me last night!

But as he blinked the sleep out of his eyes, he was relieved to find his father bending over him.

"Da?" John Huggins almost never left the stokers' realm in the nether regions of the *Titanic*. Since sailing day, Alfie had seen his father only once or twice outside the orange-black glow of Number 5 Boiler Room.

The ash-stained face looked haunted. "Alfie, how do you know that boy?"

"Boy? What boy?"

"He brought water to the black gang yesterday," his father prodded. "He spoke to me — mentioned you by name. He was in the firemen's quarters just now, but he's not one of us. What's he to you?"

Alfie chose to play innocent, but his heart was sinking. He'd always feared that his association with Paddy would come to light. "I don't know who you mean," he lied. "There are many young crew members. Sometimes even the steerage boys help out for a few coins."

John Huggins looked worried. "I hope to God you're telling the truth, lad. There's talk of a stowaway. And if you've aided him, it's both our jobs. Where would we ever find work again with a blot like that on our records?"

With a growing sense of dread, the young steward

realized that his father was right. Alfie's own rash behavior and Paddy's carelessness threatened to bring down all of them. New York was still some three days away. How would he ever keep this awful secret until then?

He felt the bulkheads of the crew quarters closing in on him.

CHAPTER FOURTEEN

RMS *TITANIC*
SUNDAY, APRIL 14, 1912, 7:45 A.M.

Rodney, Earl of Glamford, was never pleasant in the morning. This was usually thanks to his gaming losses and the crashing headache he suffered due to overindulging the night before.

Yet this morning, Juliana entered the parlor of their suite to find her father in a towering rage.

"I require an explanation of your behavior, miss!" he demanded harshly.

"I have no idea what you mean, Papa."

"Do you not?" he raged. "Before you craft a proper lie, you should know that I witnessed your disgusting display — down in steerage, no less!"

Juliana worked hard to keep her expression neutral. Papa must not be allowed to see her humiliation at being exposed indulging in a pastime unbecoming the daughter of an earl. Amid the chaos of last night and her worry over what might have happened to

Paddy, the one thing she thought she'd known for certain was that her father would be deep in a card game, oblivious to it all.

Alas, not so.

The old Juliana would have held her peace and taken the tongue-lashing meekly. But she was not the same girl that she had been at the start of this voyage. Her friendship with Sophie — and with Alfie and Paddy, too — had opened her eyes. Instead of blindly following a code of conduct that was centuries old, why not accept people of all stations with an open heart, and take kindness where you find it? In spite of the upsets of last night, she still remembered the glow of being welcomed into the third-class celebration.

"How peculiar," she ventured demurely, "that in spite of your concern at my behavior, you were not waiting here in the cabin when I returned."

"How dare you?" he retorted. "So distressed was I at the sight of you flouncing around like a common scullery maid that I required some companionship to settle my nerves!"

"Fifty-two companions, no doubt. That is, I believe, the number of cards in a deck."

Enraged, he raised a hand to her, but thought better of it when she stood her ground and did not flinch. When he spoke again, his voice was softer, but no less angry. "Stupid girl, there are factors at play here that you cannot possibly begin to grasp."

For some reason, she thought of Sophie's mother — Amelia Bronson's outrage at being denied the vote. Until this moment, Juliana had not seen what was so important about casting a ballot for a prime minister you would probably never meet. Now she understood perfectly. What galled Mrs. Bronson — what should gall all women — was the belief that no female was intelligent enough to make her own decisions.

"Then please enlighten me," she told her father. "I am not feeble-minded. Tell me of these 'factors.'"

"Did you consider what would happen should Mr. Hardcastle hear of your dancing with swirling skirts?" challenged the earl.

"Mr. Hardcastle?" Juliana repeated. "Your business associate is not aboard the *Titanic*!"

"Do you not think these Americans gossip and spread rumors like fishwives?" her father exploded. "The entirety of what they call society is aboard this vessel!"

She lowered her gaze. "I should regret to cause you embarrassment, Papa. But I fail to see how my conduct could have any effect on your commerce with a man who owns oil wells."

"Then you are extremely shortsighted. Hardcastle

may be an American, but he will care very much about the reputation of the future bride of one of his sons!"

"*Bride?*" Juliana was rocked back on her heels. "I'm fifteen years old!"

"In less than two years, you will be seventeen and marriageable. Mr. Hardcastle has three sons. Not many girls get such a choice."

"I choose none of them!" Juliana exclaimed, horrified.

"I warned you that you would not understand. Perhaps you do not notice the financial difficulties of your family because you are still kept in silks and satins. Hardcastle has all the money in the world, but only you can place his family within the nobility."

"So now I have children, too?" Juliana sputtered.

"It is your duty to rescue your family," her father lectured. "That is what young ladies of your station are called upon to do. And if they are well-bred, they do it gladly."

Juliana had a brief vision of her mother weeping uncontrollably on the dock at Southampton as the *Titanic* sailed.

She knows! Everybody knows — except me!

At that moment, Juliana would have preferred to hang rather than let her father see her cry. But the tears came. She could not hold them back. She stumbled to the stateroom door and threw it open.

"When you invited me to accompany you on this business trip," she sobbed, "you neglected to mention that *I* was the merchandise to be bartered!"

She ran blindly along the passageway, wanting only to get away from him. Never before had she felt so completely betrayed or so utterly alone. Here she was, half an ocean away from the only home she had ever known, her sole companion the father who had put her up for sale to finance his gambling debts and pay for his polo ponies, aeroplanes, and other toys. Who knew if she'd ever see her mother again? She wasn't even certain she wanted to. What sort of parent would send her only child off on a voyage of no return? Yes, she had wept on the dock. But her sadness had not given her the courage and decency to warn her daughter of her impending fate.

Nobody cares what happens to me. . . .

She pulled up short, dashing the tears from her eyes with a balled fist. Someone did care. She thought back to the day she and Sophie had found Paddy hiding in the linen drawer under her bed. His exact words: *All that blather about your reputation — what I'm saying, miss, is there's something not quite right about it.*

His background could not have been more opposite to hers, but *Paddy* cared. He had tried to
warn her.

I've got to speak with him!

Of course, she had no way of knowing where Paddy
was right now — especially after last night's hue and
cry. But Alfie had told her that the stowaway had a
secret hiding place in one of the Astors' trunks in the
baggage hold.

If she were to find Paddy, it would probably be
there.

Second Officer Lightoller was on the enclosed B-Deck
promenade when he heard the sobs. He prided himself on being a no-nonsense seaman. Yet an officer
did not sail with the cream of British and American
society without knowing a thing or two about service. Aboard the *Titanic*, an unhappy first-class
passenger might well have friends in very high places
indeed — in Parliament, in Congress, or perhaps even
within the royal family itself.

But when he located the source of the lament, he
stood back. It was young Lady Juliana, her face pink
and tear-streaked. He could well imagine why. No
doubt her father had torn a strip off her after her
behavior at the party in steerage.

Lightoller's lips thinned into a straight line. That was the second time Miss Glamm had been found in close proximity to the stowaway. He would have loved to question her on the subject. But one did not interrogate the daughter of the Earl of Glamford like a common criminal. Not aboard the crown jewel of the White Star Line.

As he watched, Juliana's expression changed from tragic to determined, and she began to move along the promenade — long strides that bristled with purpose. He followed at a distance.

She took the outside staircase down to the well deck and entered the forecastle at C Deck. Lightoller was intrigued. The girl was now in the working part of the ship, and she seemed to know exactly where she was going.

Without slowing, the second officer pulled an able seaman out of a huddle of crew. "Come with me."

The sailor fell into step beside him. "Where are we going, sir?"

"We'll know soon enough."

At a brisk pace, Juliana headed forward to the Number 2 Hatch and started down the spiral stairs, her footfalls reverberating softly on the metal.

"Fancy lady to be mucking around the lower

decks," the sailor commented as Juliana descended into the bowels of the ship.

"She has a nose for trouble, this one," Lightoller agreed. "Now hold your tongue."

He watched as Juliana left the stairs on the orlop deck and disappeared among the first- and second-class baggage. The two seamen trailed after her, walking lightly to avoid betraying their pursuit. Keeping to the cover of the larger piles of luggage, they crept closer.

Lightoller peered around a stack of leather cases. His eyes narrowed as the girl opened the lid of an enormous steamer trunk. A head and shoulders sat up into view.

The second officer sprang into action.

Juliana spied them first. "Run, Paddy!"

But she was too late. Lightoller grabbed the cover-alled figure by one arm; the sailor took hold of the other. The two men lifted the struggling Paddy out of the trunk and set him on the deck, firmly under their control.

"Well, now," said the second officer of the *Titanic*, "do you know what we do with stowaways in His Majesty's merchant service?"

CHAPTER FIFTEEN

RMS *TITANIC*
SUNDAY, APRIL 14, 1912, 8:15 A.M.

"What have we here?" rumbled Kevin Gilhooley with a cruel smile. "If you put out enough rubbish, sooner or later you'll trap a rat."

The gangster and his henchman, Seamus, watched from behind the bars of their cells as Lightoller and Master-at-Arms King shoved Paddy into a chair.

Lightoller ignored the prisoners and skewered the stowaway with burning eyes. "I'll have your name, boy, and the name of the crewman who let you board this ship."

Paddy stuck out his chin. "Patrick Burns. And nobody let me aboard."

The second officer reddened. "So the angels brought you down from heaven above?"

"No angels. It was your own cargo crane that plucked me off the dock in Belfast. Hiding in a bale of linen, I was" — he pointed at the two gangsters in the brig — "from this murdering scum!"

"Put the lad in here with me," Gilhooley suggested. "And I'll gladly save you the trouble of what to do with him when we get to New York."

"Shut your gob," King ordered.

Lightoller was astounded. "Are you telling me that you've been aboard the *Titanic* for *twelve days*? Living *where*? Not in that box! Who's been feeding you? Miss Glamm obviously, but she's only been aboard since Southampton. You have an accomplice — someone of the crew. Is it young Huggins?"

"Don't know the man."

"You mentioned his name to me!"

His captive stared back defiantly. "If I can hide aboard your precious ship for twelve days, grant me the guile to parrot back a name I've heard."

"Don't lie to me!" The second officer raised his arm to strike.

Paddy had already resolved that, no matter what happened, he would not betray Alfie. If he had to take a beating from Lightoller, so be it. He had suffered worse at the hand of his stepfather. And poor Daniel had suffered far, far worse from the two men on the other side of the bars of the brig.

"Don't you see that the boy is at the root of both our problems?" Gilhooley reasoned. "Surely we can come to an arrangement. Release me and I'll have the information you need in five minutes."

Lightoller looked from Gilhooley to Paddy, and then to the master-at-arms. "Lock the thugs up together, and put the boy in the other cell. I don't want him harmed until I've had a chance to interrogate him."

☆

"Here's your hot chocolate, Miss Sophie." Alfie handed her a steaming mug. "Would you like me to get you a blanket? They say the temperature is dropping rapidly."

Sophie seemed distracted. She barely noticed the chill of the boat deck as she accepted the drink and took a sip. "I'd like to talk to him!" she blurted suddenly.

"Him?" Alfie repeated, puzzled.

"Mr. Masterson. It breaks my heart to see how lonely he is."

Alfie bit his lip. "You must be joking! No one wants to talk to Mr. Masterson. I wish I didn't have to! And he's taken a liking to me, more's the pity."

"I hope you didn't borrow that attitude from my mother," Sophie said disapprovingly. "Just because she's Amelia Bronson doesn't mean she's always right."

"I'm not saying she's always right," Alfie returned. "But she's right this time."

"How could you be so unfeeling?" Sophie accused. "The poor soul has been so isolated by the loss of his legs that he's unable to be sociable. He needs to be accepted by the rest of us, not forced further into the darkness. I want to be introduced to him. At least I can make the remainder of this voyage more pleasant for him."

"You'll not go near the man," Alfie said grimly.

Sophie frowned. "I didn't ask for your permission. You're my steward and you're his steward. Who better to make the introduction?"

Alfie remained stubborn. "I'll not do it."

Sophie faced him with growing annoyance. "Very well. I'll introduce myself. I'm a modern woman. I don't have to worry about the outdated customs of the last century."

She handed him back the mug and turned to leave.

"No, wait! Listen," Alfie pleaded.

"I see no reason why I should," Sophie said coldly.

Alfie took a deep breath. There was no choice but to tell all. "Remember the scrapbook I showed you and Miss Juliana in the baggage hold? The one about the Whitechapel murders? It belongs to Mr. Masterson."

"I can believe that," Sophie replied thoughtfully. "Keeping a scrapbook would be one of the few pastimes available to an invalid. And in light of his misfortune, it's understandable that he might develop an interest in a dark subject, like a series of —" She pulled up short. "Alfie, you're *not* saying that crippled old man is Jack the Ripper?"

"He wasn't old and crippled then," Alfie reasoned. "He was injured in 1889 — when the Whitechapel murders ended. That's why Jack the Ripper stopped killing! He wasn't physically capable of it anymore." He grasped Sophie's arm. "As your steward — as your *friend* — I can't let you go to him. Your mother is right — he does hate women."

Sophie was flustered, but she had Amelia Bronson's rock-solid faith in her own convictions. "There must be another explanation. It's only a scrapbook —"

"With teeth?" Alfie challenged.

"We can't know for certain —"

The exchange was interrupted when Juliana barreled up to them, agitated in the extreme.

"Paddy's under arrest and it's all my fault!" she blurted, her pink cheeks streaked with tears.

"What?" chorused Alfie and Sophie.

Juliana began to cry again as she told them how she had inadvertently led Lightoller to Paddy's hiding place in the baggage hold. "I tried to stop him," she panted, out of breath from running up to the boat deck. "But Mr. Lightoller said that hiding Paddy is almost as serious as stowing away yourself, and I might be arrested, too!"

"He's bluffing!" Sophie scoffed. "The White Star Line would never do that to a first-class passenger, certainly not the daughter of an earl."

Alfie went pale, remembering the conversation with his father early that morning. "But they won't hesitate to do it to a junior steward! At the least, I'll be fired, and my poor father, too, for helping me!"

"He *didn't* help you!" Juliana exclaimed, aghast.

"Begging your pardon, miss, but the respect and consideration you're used to — that's just not how the world works for people like Da and me. The White Star Line has the power of the Lord on high over us, and we can be sacked at any time for any reason, or for no reason at all, if that's the captain's pleasure. I'm not so much worried for myself as for my father. He's been with White Star well nigh twenty years. A man his age with no other job experience — he'd starve, and probably me with him!"

Both girls regarded him with pity. The life he

described was completely foreign to them. Yet they could see in his haunted eyes that he was telling them the truth.

"What can be done?" Sophie asked anxiously.

"I can't be connected to Paddy," Alfie reasoned. "Which means I can't risk being seen with you two. As your steward, of course. But as friends — that's just not possible anymore." He regarded Juliana ruefully. "I suppose you were right all along, Miss Julie. It's not a good idea for the classes to mix socially."

She shook her head sadly. "I was ever so wrong."

Alfie looked around the boat deck, his expression wary. "I should go. Don't do anything rash to try to save Paddy. He's at the mercy of the White Star Line now. It's possible that I am, too — and my poor father." He hurried away, leaving the two girls standing at the rail, forlorn.

"I could never have imagined how much I shall miss his company," Juliana said tragically.

"He's not dead," Sophie pointed out. "He just has to be careful around us, that's all. What on earth possessed you to decide that you had to go to the hold and find Paddy this morning?"

Juliana felt the tears returning and steeled herself with a deep breath. "That's the worst part of this. I learned the real reason for this voyage to America."

Sophie was confused. "It isn't your father's business?"

"It is. But the nature of that business is to barter me to the son of an oil tycoon." In halting speech, she told of her father's plan to marry her to one of Mr. Hardcastle's sons in order to rescue the Glamm family's finances. "He says it's my duty as his daughter," she finished miserably.

Sophie was horrified. "A hundred years ago, perhaps! Not in the twentieth century!"

"But what can *I* do about it?"

"Women are never as powerless as men want us to think we are," Sophie lectured. "And that comes straight from my mother, the world's greatest bigmouth on the subject of women's rights. Julie, they can put you on a ship to America. They can even dress you in white lace and a veil and drag you to the altar. But they can't make you say yes."

"Of course they can," Juliana sniffed.

Sophie shook her head. "They can bribe you, browbeat you, shout until they're blue in the face. But in the end, that final measure of control is yours and yours alone. Let's talk to Mother. She can help."

"Then let her help Paddy," Juliana said adamantly. "He's the one who really needs it right now. It doesn't matter what happens to me."

CHAPTER SIXTEEN

RMS *TITANIC*
SUNDAY, APRIL 14, 1912, 2:15 P.M.

"Five hundred forty-six miles in a single day!" marveled J. Bruce Ismay. "Most impressive! At this speed, a Tuesday night arrival is almost assured!"

The managing director of the White Star Line stood in his usual place next to Captain Smith on the bridge of the *Titanic*.

Thomas Andrews was buried in a page of mathematical calculations. "The degree of steam pressure with all twenty-nine boilers engaged is quite different from my estimates."

The captain cast him a wry look. "Better or worse?"

"Higher," the designer replied. "Of course, faster is not necessarily better."

"It will be when the newspapers are trumpeting our name," Ismay put in. "Much better."

First Officer Murdoch escorted a visitor into the captain's presence. "Mrs. Bronson to see you, sir."

"Good day to you, madam," Captain Smith greeted pleasantly. "What brings you to my bridge?"

Amelia Bronson was not one to waste time on small talk. "You have a child in your brig, one Patrick Burns."

Second Officer Lightoller spoke up. "I put him there myself. The boy is a stowaway."

"Not anymore." Mrs. Bronson opened her silk purse. "I wish to purchase third-class passage for him. Now he is a paid passenger like the rest of us."

"I'm afraid the time for that is past, madam," the captain explained gently. "A stowaway is a thief as surely as if he has purloined silverware from the dining saloon. Paying for his theft does not absolve him of the original crime."

"He is a child," the suffragist persisted.

"Maritime law makes no allowance for youth," Smith told her. "The boy will be treated humanely, but he will be prosecuted for his offense."

Mrs. Bronson emitted a most unladylike snort of disgust. "Maritime law! Just another excuse for men to bully the weakest among us — women and children."

"My dear lady!" the captain protested. "Surely you know that Maritime law places the utmost value upon the safety of women and children!"

"My apologies, madam." Wireless Operator Phillips stepped around Mrs. Bronson and held a message slip out to the captain. "From the *Baltic*, sir. Reporting large quantities of pack ice, latitude 41°51' N, longitude 49°52' W."

"That's about two hundred miles ahead of us," Lightoller supplied.

Captain Smith preferred not to discuss ship's business when there was a lady present. That was how rumors began. "Is that all, Mr. Phillips?"

"It's possible that we missed a few others while the equipment was down," the operator admitted.

Frowning, the captain accepted the paper and passed it, unread, to Ismay.

The managing director didn't read it, either.

The Grand Staircase was Sophie's favorite part of the *Titanic*. It wasn't just beautiful; it was *startling* in its beauty. How many times had she stood in this very spot — on the C-Deck landing, looking down upon the reception area outside the first-class saloon? The magnificent stained-glass dome overhead was turned luminous by the dusk. The gathering diners seemed to glow, as if nature itself had cast a spotlight upon these special and celebrated people.

That evening, Julie was with her father. Now that his awful plan was in jeopardy, the earl had remembered he had a daughter. And Mother was in second class, trying to organize a group of suffrage converts. Sophie was on her own — an unescorted young lady in an evening gown. Not long ago, it would have been a scandal. But this was an amazing new century of wireless messages, electric lights, and unsinkable ships. So much progress in a few short years! What the future might hold, no one could imagine.

She spied Alfie, who was settling Mr. Masterson into a chair in the reception area. She gave the young steward a small wave, but he was studiously ignoring her. So that was how it was going to be, she reflected glumly. Poor Alfie. He couldn't risk being associated with her, and therefore Juliana, and therefore Paddy. She understood, yet it saddened her just the same.

Mr. Masterson was being irascible, as usual, growling with a sour face, and actually poking Alfie with his crutch when he was ready to be left alone. What a truly disagreeable person! But Jack the

Ripper? That had to be Alfie's overactive imagination. Surely there was another explanation for that scrapbook.

I'm going to get to the bottom of it, Sophie promised herself.

Her long gown swept gracefully down the carpeted stairs as she descended to the reception room. She seated herself across from the old man and held out her hand. "Good evening, Mr. Masterson. I'm Sophie Bronson."

He made no move to take it. "I know who you are," he said with a scowl. "You're the daughter of that god-awful suffragette."

Sophie bristled. "The term is 'suffragist.' "

"*Renegade* would be a better word. What else would you call a shameless rabble-rouser bent on overturning the natural order of things?"

She burned at the insult to her mother, but resisted the urge to walk away. She had no right to be surprised that this man was unpleasant. Passengers and crew had been complaining about him ever since the ship had left Southampton.

"I'll be blunt, sir," she said, mustering her nerve. It was not every day that you asked a gentleman to explain that he was *not* Jack the Ripper. "A scrapbook belonging to you was found loose in the baggage hold — a detailed chronicle of the Whitechapel murders of 1888 —"

"Found?" Masterson's eyes widened. "By whom?"

"I found it myself," Sophie lied. She could not risk making more trouble for Alfie. "I was searching for a hatbox when I noticed it had fallen out of your trunk."

"Who else knows of this?" he demanded. "Did you tell any member of the crew?"

Sophie shook her head. "I don't wish to cause you any embarrassment. But I'm interested to know why you would own such a thing. I realize that your life is hard and that your legs cause you constant pain. Yet how does that explain your fascination with such terrible crimes?"

Masterson peered into her eyes, taking her measure. "I shall give you the explanation you seek," he said at last.

Sophie sat back expectantly.

"Not here," he added. "Not with these eavesdropping vipers all around. You alone understand the misery that is my world, and this account is for you alone. Meet me on the forecastle deck after dinner."

"The forecastle deck?" Sophie echoed in surprise. "Isn't that an awfully long walk for you?"

"I must exercise continually lest I lose the use of

my legs altogether. I prefer the late hours when I don't have to navigate around rich fools at every step. Shall we say eleven thirty?" Before she could answer, he added, "Dress warmly, Miss Bronson. I hear the night is going to be extremely cold."

CHAPTER SEVENTEEN

RMS *TITANIC*
Sunday, April 14, 1912, 11:25 p.m.

When the hand closed on his sleeve, Alfie was so shocked that he nearly dropped a full-length chinchilla wrap that cost more than the pay of a junior steward for twenty years. He wheeled around to see Juliana skulking in the shadows of the open A-Deck promenade, hugging herself against the chill.

"Miss Julie!" Alfie exclaimed. "You gave me a fright!"

"I'm trying to be discreet about our friendship," she whispered, "as you requested."

"One of the fellows asked me to bring this wrap to Mr. Guggenheim's companion," Alfie told her. "If I damage it, I might as well jump over the rail."

"I apologize for startling you," said Juliana. "And I apologize for getting Paddy arrested and for casting suspicion upon you. Honestly, at this moment, I can't think of a single thing in my life that I'm *not* sorry about. My father, certainly."

"I see he is back to his card game in the lounge."

She nodded. "I knew his concern for my reputation wouldn't distract him long from his first love. And Sophie is off with your Mr. Masterson —"

"Masterson?" This time Alfie really did drop the fur wrap. He scrambled to pick it up. "Why?"

Juliana shrugged. "He's her project. She thinks showing him kindness will civilize the man. She's becoming a crusader like her mother."

"Where?" Alfie barked urgently. "Did she say where they were meeting?"

"The forecastle deck. He takes a late walk to —"

Alfie did not wait for her to finish the sentence. He turned tail and pounded along the promenade, disappearing down a forward passageway.

The chinchilla wrap lay discarded on the deck.

By day, the forecastle of the *Titanic* thronged with activity; by night it was a broad, deserted battlement.

No, not deserted, Sophie reminded herself as she climbed the stairs from the well deck. To her left towered the base of the foremast. High above, she knew, were two lookouts in the crow's nest. And, of course, Mr. Masterson was here somewhere.

There was little protection from the bitter cold wind, and she shivered beneath her cloak. Mr. Masterson's choice of meeting place was as odd as his choice of topic for a hobby scrapbook. But all that would be revealed soon enough.

She spied a figure leaning on a crutch at the rail. "Mr. Masterson?"

"Come here, child, and observe. The sea is flat as glass." The voice was gruff, yet the tone was friendly.

He can be nice when people are nice to him.

She joined him. "Like a mirror," she agreed. "You can even see the reflection of the stars."

She waited expectantly, smiling up into his weathered face. He had promised her an explanation. When none came, she prompted gently, "You were going to tell me about the scrapbook."

In answer, he reached out and seized her with a grip of startling power. "Stupid daughter of a stupid mother! Not to recognize the evidence of your own eyes! That scrapbook is not a hobby! It's a celebration of my masterpiece!"

Sophie tried to scream but an iron hand clamped over her mouth. This seemingly helpless cripple had the strength of ten men in his arms. Her feeble struggles were in vain as he pressed her against the rail. With her body now immobilized, he reached inside his breast pocket and drew out a shadowy object. Shiny steel reflected the distant lights of the *Titanic*'s superstructure.

Sophie's eyes widened in horror. It was a hunting knife with a long, serrated blade.

Mr. Masterson was triumphant. "For twenty-four years, my work has been stifled by these worthless legs, but no longer!" The knife came toward her. At the last second, a delicate twist cut the string of pearls from her around throat. "So my scrapbook is of interest to you! Perhaps it will be some consolation that *you* will grace the latest page! These baubles will be my memento!"

"You'll be caught!" Sophie breathed. "You'll hang!"

His smile was cruel. "I don't think so. You're such a little thing" — all at once, she felt her feet leave the deck as he lifted her up and over the rail — "and the ocean is so large."

She tried to call for help, but could only manage a terrified gasp.

CHAPTER EIGHTEEN

RMS *TITANIC*
SUNDAY, APRIL 14, 1912, 11:39 P.M.

Forty-five feet up, in the crow's nest, lookouts Frederick Fleet and Reginald Lee were completely unaware of the drama taking place below them on the forecastle deck. Their eyes were scanning the Atlantic ahead.

The night was clear, the sea perfectly calm, but this only made their job more difficult. With no wave action, it would be impossible to spot a large berg by the white water at the base. Worse, there was no moon at all. Fleet hoped that the thousands of stars out tonight would provide enough light to see the approach of the ice that had been reported in the shipping lanes.

Symons, the previous lookout, insisted that "you can smell the ice before you get to it." Fleet hoped so. Right now, he smelled — and saw — nothing.

And then the emptiness *moved*.

He blinked. Something lay ahead, something darker than the night. How was that possible? In the next moment, he knew all too well. An immense form was approaching, blocking the stars as it drew closer.

There was only one possible explanation.

He rang the crow's nest bell three times — the signal for danger. Heart pounding, he picked up the telephone to the wheelhouse. "Is anyone there?" he rasped.

On the bridge, Sixth Officer Moody answered the call. "What do you see?"

"Iceberg right ahead."

"*Iceberg right ahead!*" Moody bawled to First Officer Murdoch, who was in command.

"Hard a' starboard!" shouted Murdoch. Even as he gave the order, he ran for the engine room telegraph, signaling *full speed astern*. The way to stop a moving ship was to throw the screws into reverse.

At the helm, Quartermaster Hichens twirled the wheel hard over, twisting his body as if the shifting of his weight might somehow coax the huge ocean liner to turn more quickly.

The five crew members on the bridge stared anxiously out over the prow, waiting for the nose of the ship to swing away from the menacing black shape that blocked their path.

☆

Alfie pounded up the stairs from the well deck and peered urgently around the darkened forecastle. The electric lights of the bow were shut off for the overnight hours to aid the lookouts in the crow's nest.

A faint cry — more of a whimper — reached his ears, and he pivoted in the direction of the sound. The sight that met his eyes very nearly stopped his heart.

Mr. Masterson had Sophie against the rail — half over it, in fact. In his right hand he wielded a vicious looking saw-toothed knife.

Alfie ran blindly, wildly, with no clear plan in his mind except to stop this latest Whitechapel murder twenty-four years after the fact. He grabbed the knife arm, straining to direct the weapon away from Sophie.

"*You!*" Masterson seethed, concentrating his considerable force on the tug-of-war with Alfie.

The blade began to move, slowly yet inexorably, toward Sophie's throat. Alfie pulled with all his might, grunting with the effort to stop the knife's deadly progress. It was no use. He thought back to the *Titanic*'s gymnasium — the man's almost supernatural upper-body strength.

I'll never overpower him this way. . . .

Out of options, Alfie reared back his foot and slammed it into the crippled man's knee.

The howl of agony that came from Mr. Masterson was barely human. He went down like a sack of oats, his crutch flailing above him. The knife clattered to the deck.

"Alfie!" Now free of the killer's hold, Sophie was rolling over the top of the rail, completely untethered to the ship.

Alfie lunged, barely getting his hands around her waist before she fell. He hauled her back aboard and the two of them collapsed in a heap.

"Are you all right?" Alfie rasped.

Sophie pointed, her face full of dread. Mr. Masterson was on his feet once more, leaning heavily on his crutch. In his hand was a small black revolver.

The gun was pointed at them.

In the crow's nest, lookouts Fleet and Lee heard voices below, but their attention never wavered from the approaching iceberg, now just off the *Titanic*'s bow.

Why doesn't she turn? Fleet thought desperately. It seemed an eternity since he'd telephoned his warning to the wheelhouse.

On the bridge, First Officer Murdoch understood all too well. The world's largest ocean liner could not be steered like a team of horses. He had silently counted thirty seconds, and still the ship was steaming directly toward the obstacle.

Finally the prow began to swerve to port. The forepeak pivoted away from the berg, and suddenly the mountain of ice was passing them close on the starboard side.

Murdoch held his breath. Had they made it?

Masterson's words came out in halting gasps, but his arm was ramrod straight as he held the pistol on Alfie and Sophie. "Do you honestly think," he puffed in outrage, "that I'd let a meddling lackey and a silly wench come between me and my destiny?"

"What destiny?" Alfie shot back. "To kill people? To be Jack the Ripper again?"

"*I was always he!*" Masterson stormed. "Don't let this broken body deceive you! If my operation is successful, my work can resume! Just think of it — a new country in which I shall continue my great quest. But I'm afraid you two will not be there to see it." There was a click as he released the safety catch of his revolver. "It is not my weapon of choice. But for an old cripple, simplicity is important. Useless legs cannot hinder the effectiveness of a bullet. Nothing can, I'm afraid. . . ."

So focused was Alfie on the barrel of Masterson's gun that he nearly missed what happened next. An enormous blue-black mountain came up on the starboard bow. For a moment, the *Titanic* seemed to vibrate, a grinding sensation from deep within the ship. Far below the waterline, a spur of ice scraped against the hull, buckling the metal plating. Rivets popped by the thousands, allowing the relentless sea to rush inside under pressure. In Number 6 Boiler Room, the bulkhead suddenly vanished, to be replaced by a torrent of frigid ocean that washed out the stokers and sent shovelfuls of coal flying.

Up on the forecastle, a series of sharp cracks sounded as chunks of shattered ice broke from the berg. They struck the deck and tumbled across the polished hardwood. One of them knocked the crutch out from under Masterson's weight, and the crippled man went down hard.

Alfie did not hesitate. He hurled himself at the fallen assailant and clamped his hands onto the gun still clenched in Masterson's hand. But the killer recovered quickly, twisting the weapon so that the barrel was pointing at the young steward's face.

A split second from death, Alfie's whirling thoughts turned to his mother. *You were right to fear Jack the Ripper, Mum — even all these years after Whitechapel. . . .*

Sophie's pink satin slipper slammed into the pistol, sending it skittering under the rail. It dropped to the well deck with a clunk.

Alfie heard Masterson's enraged roar, followed by a brutal slap, and Sophie's cry of pain. Then he saw the crutch swinging toward the side of his head.

Explosion of impact, blinding light.

Darkness.

CHAPTER NINETEEN

On the bridge, the collision was nothing remarkable — a brief grating jar that replaced the steady vibration of the engines for a few seconds. But there was no mistaking the iceberg, towering one hundred feet out of the water, passing on the starboard side. Immediately, Murdoch threw the switch to close the watertight doors.

In Number 5 Boiler Room, the cascade of in-rushing water was so loud that John Huggins barely noticed the alarm bell until the iron hatch began to lower. Stokers, drenched and bellowing, leaped, scrambled, and crawled through the passage from Number 6. One fireman slipped on the slick deck and flopped on his face, inches from being crushed by the descending metal. Huggins grabbed his wrist and pulled him through just as the heavy door locked into place. The bulkhead was sealed, but the gash in the hull extended well past it, the sea pouring into the belly of the *Titanic*.

At that moment, Captain E. J. Smith rushed onto the bridge to a barrage of reports about the nature of the accident. The experienced seaman listened grimly. It was entirely possible that, by reversing the engines, his first officer had made a grave error. A large liner was most maneuverable when she was moving the fastest. If the *Titanic* had maintained speed, she might have missed the iceberg altogether.

Smith did not say this aloud, of course. Any sailor worth his salt knew that the past was past. All that mattered was the here and now. How serious was the damage?

No one yet knew.

"Ask the carpenter to sound the ship," he ordered. "And summon Mr. Andrews."

Alfie awoke to a throbbing in his head and a burning cold against his jaw. When he opened his eyes, he saw Sophie, kneeling over him, her face bruised and anxious, holding a brick-sized piece of ice to his cheek.

Ice . . . the berg . . .

"Jack the Ripper!" he exclaimed, sitting up suddenly. "Where did he go?"

"He limped off. Oh, Alfie, you were so right! He tried to kill me!"

Alfie shook his head to clear it. "This time he's well and truly caught. The *Titanic* isn't Whitechapel, where he can disappear down a sewer. And tonight we have a live witness."

Sophie nodded feelingly. "It's a lucky thing that iceberg came along, or he would have finished the both of us!"

Alfie took stock of their surroundings. Blocks and chips of ice lay strewn about the forecastle. "I thought there would be more," he commented. "I felt the whole ship shake."

"I've read that the bulk of an iceberg is underwater," Sophie put in. "Maybe most of the shaking took place belowdecks."

Alfie looked worried. "I think I should go down and check on my da."

"But what about Jack the Ripper?" Sophie protested in a voice writhing with anxiety. "He's loose on the ship! We have to tell the officers before he attacks somebody else!"

"Come with me as far as E Deck," Alfie decided. "That's Scotland Road. There's always a lot of crew around. Someone will know what to do."

They descended to the well deck and reentered the forecastle to the spiral staircase.

"Listen," Sophie urged.

Alfie paused. "I don't hear anything."

"That's just it. From the moment we left Southampton, the thrum of the engines was as natural as your own heartbeat. Now it's stopped. You don't suppose anything's really wrong, do you?"

Alfie quickened their pace on the metal stairs. "My father will know. He's worked on ships all his life."

As they approached E Deck, the hustle and bustle of Scotland Road reached their ears. If anything, it seemed more active than usual to Alfie. "I'll come find you once I've spoken with my da."

She started to go, then turned to him, eyes huge. "Alfie, you saved my life."

"And you saved mine right back," he told her. "I'll see you soon."

He continued down, hurrying now, the silence of the engines preying on his mind. Now he was aware of a cold, damp wind rising from below. Why had he never noticed that before?

As he neared the bottom, an appalling sight met his unbelieving gaze. Dark water swirled at the base of the staircase. Shocked, he climbed back up to F Deck and threaded his way aft to the ladder access to the boiler rooms.

As he descended, unimaginable chaos enveloped him. The wind was even stronger, only here it churned thick with steam and smoke. The stokers, some drenched from head to toe, splashed around in knee-deep water. And the noise was unavoidable — a cacophony of urgent bellowed instructions to "Shut the dampers!" "Man the pumps!" and "Don't let the water reach the furnaces!"

"Da!" It was no use. Alfie's shouts were lost in the pandemonium. He dropped to the deck, the frigid water soaking his thighs. It was so cold that it doubled his heartbeat, and raised his voice by an octave. *"Da!"*

He began to slog toward Number 5, jostled by the tumult of activity. Finally, an engineer recognized him and relieved John Huggins at a pump.

"Boy, you should be with your passengers!" His father's voice was exhausted.

"What's going on, Da?"

"She's making water! We must have struck something — a smaller ship perhaps. That happened to the *Olympic*."

Alfie shook his head. "It was an iceberg. But how would that create wind?"

"All this water coming in, it pushes the air up and out."

The young steward regarded him in alarm. "Is the ship seriously damaged?"

"They say she's unsinkable." John Huggins looked grim. "It looks like we're going to find out. Now, get to your passengers. Rich ladies don't like to be disturbed in the middle of their beauty sleep."

"I won't leave you here!" Alfie protested.

"I've a job to do, lad — and so have you. *Go!*"

Halfway up the access ladder, Alfie turned, irresistibly drawn back to his father. John Huggins was on the pump once more, manning his post as he always had. As a breadwinner, he'd provided neither wealth nor luxury, only long lonely absences that had ultimately driven his wife away. Still, he was a father to be proud of, to admire. For some reason, Alfie had trouble tearing his gaze away.

No sooner had he set his feet on F Deck than he was nearly bowled over by a running figure. Struggling to stay upright, he recognized one of the clerks from the post office.

The young man was soaking wet and distraught. "The mail room is swamped!"

Alfie was shocked. How could that be? The mail was sorted on G — just a deck below where they were now. "How much water?"

"The packages are floating!"

"The captain must be informed!" Alfie exclaimed.

"Informed of what?" came a calm voice from behind them. Fourth Officer Boxhall approached, his sharp eyes taking note of their dripping uniforms and frantic expressions.

"Four feet of water in the mail room, sir!" the clerk gasped. "And it's worse farther forward! Escaping air has blown the hatch off the forepeak tank!"

"Move as much of the mail as you can up to F Deck," Boxhall ordered. To Alfie, he said, "Put on dry clothing before seeing to your passengers. We don't want any rumors that something is amiss."

"But" — Alfie could scarcely believe his ears — "something *is* amiss!"

The fourth officer smiled thinly. "Don't be absurd, lad. Nothing is amiss until the captain says it is."

CHAPTER TWENTY

RMS *TITANIC*
SUNDAY, APRIL 14, 1912, 11:45 P.M.

To Juliana in stateroom B-56, the collision had felt like a gentle scrape — merely a brief interruption in the ship's smooth progress. Moments later, there was a stir of voices in the passageway — polite questions from the first-class passengers and reassuring replies from their stewards.

"There's talk of an iceberg, miss," Junior Steward Tryhorn told Juliana. "I'm sure they'll get it sorted out soon enough."

Most went back to bed, but a few intrepid souls wrapped themselves in overcoats and ventured out to see if they could catch a glimpse of this Atlantic novelty.

By the time Juliana made it up to the A-Deck promenade, there was no berg to be seen. But looking down, she could tell that the well deck and forecastle were littered with ice fragments. A few young tuxedo-clad first-class men had organized an impromptu football match with the larger chunks, and were creating quite an uproar in their mirth. The scene reminded her of stories she had heard of Papa in his youth — mindless, impulsive, devoted to fun. So little had changed, except that the money had run out.

It was as she returned to her suite that she encountered Alfie — drenched and disheveled. His appearance was the first sign for Juliana that all might not be well aboard the *Titanic*.

"Alfie — why are you wet?"

"I'm not supposed to alarm the passengers —" he babbled. "I've been ordered to change my clothes —"

"Does this have anything to do with the iceberg?"

"We're damaged, Miss Julie. Badly, I fear!"

"But it was only a little bump!"

"Up here, maybe," Alfie said urgently. "I've been to see my da in the boiler rooms. They're pumping like mad, but the water's still rising. Up to G Deck in the mail room!"

Juliana went suddenly white. "Where's Paddy right now?"

"The master-at-arms' office — E Deck."

"If water can reach G, it can go up to E!"

Alfie nodded. "But if there was any sign of water in the brig, I'm sure they'd move the prisoners. . . ."

Their eyes met. In that kind of emergency, would the *Titanic*'s crew have time to worry about prisoners? Or even remember the hapless souls locked in the cells, unable to move to a higher place?

"We have to see if everything is all right down there," Juliana insisted.

"I'm supposed to attend to my passengers. . . ." Alfie began.

"*I'm* one of your passengers," she insisted. "I'm going to check on Paddy."

For five days, an army of crew members had broken their necks to cater to Sophie's every whim. Now, with a killer on the loose, she couldn't find anyone to pay attention to her.

There was an abundance of crew, all of them hurrying somewhere, most of them ignoring her. A few of the kinder ones promised to seek her out and speak with her later.

"But there's a murderer on board!" she protested when Third Officer Pitman brushed her off like so many others had.

He turned and regarded her in astonishment. "My

dear young lady, it was an *iceberg*!" And he, too, rushed away.

Members of the black gang, soaked and even grimier than usual, kept climbing up from the depths of the ship, seeking out officers. High above, the mighty smokestacks began to blast their mournful foghorn calls. It wasn't so loud on Scotland Road, but on deck, it must have been earsplitting.

"Why are we blowing that horn?" she asked. "Is there another ship too close to us?"

"Just letting off steam, miss," one of the stokers called. "Pressure got too high with the engines stopped."

As she turned away, she collided with a steerage passenger who was sprinting at top speed along the passageway.

"Sorry, miss!"

He helped her up, and Sophie realized that she recognized the young man. In fact, she had danced with him at the third-class party the night before.

"Where are you going in such a rush?"

Aidan Rankin regarded her as if she were feebleminded. "Didn't you feel it? One of the boilers must have exploded!"

"We struck an iceberg," Sophie explained. "I noticed it, too. It was just a little scrape."

"Little scrape? Threw me right out of my berth, it did! Knocked me silly! And when I came to myself, there was water on the deck! I think we're sinking!"

"The *Titanic* is unsinkable," she tried to soothe.

"I've got to find Ma and my brothers!" And off he ran down Scotland Road.

A creeping unease began to take hold of Sophie — a gnawing sense that there might more peril hanging over her than the danger posed by Jack the Ripper. She decided to head back to first class and her mother. Amelia Bronson was no sailor, but she always took charge in a crisis.

Sophie rushed to the nearest staircase, took one step, and froze. Something was not right. It was almost as if the step had been *moved* — tilted ever so slightly forward. Yet that was impossible. The staircase was a fixed unit. And it looked completely level.

Still, there was that odd sensation. Had the stressful events of this night affected her mind? It had to be. Why, the only way the stair could be skewed would be if the entire ship . . .

"Sophie!"

Juliana appeared at the landing, scampering down from the upper decks, Alfie hot on her heels.

"Is it just me, or is the angle of these steps wrong?" Sophie asked them.

"The bow is filling up with water," Alfie supplied breathlessly. "Near to my waist in the boiler rooms, and entirely flooded forward of there!"

"Have you seen Paddy?" Juliana asked.

"Paddy? He's in the brig, isn't he?"

"We have to make sure he's moved somewhere safe," Alfie panted.

"But —" Sophie protested. "But the ship can't sink!"

"That won't help if the water's over his head and he's locked in!" Juliana argued.

Sophie took in the sight of Alfie's drenched uniform. "There's no water around here. I've seen wet people, but they all came up from below."

Alfie put his finger to his lips for silence. The three listened carefully. They could hear the distant roar of the smokestacks, and the hubbub of conversation from Scotland Road. But there was another sound — quieter, but steady. Almost like a draining culvert during a heavy rainstorm.

He led the girls forward. The passageway jogged to starboard around what Alfie knew to be the Number 2 Hatch. Soon, they were passing through sailors' quarters, all deserted. At this point, the full complement of crew had been called to duty by this emergency situation, which was — what? To man the pumps? What other duties might be required on an unsinkable ship?

The sound was louder now, more like a rushing river. They had reached the spiral staircase. Alfie looked down. The water sloshed around the cast-iron steps just a few feet below them. "My God, fifteen minutes ago it was still on the orlop deck!"

"It's rising quickly!" Juliana quavered. "We must find the master-at-arms and convince him to move Paddy!"

"Not yet." Alfie continued forward. Bulkheads began to curve inward as the ship's architecture narrowed near the forepeak. The passageway ended at a heavy steel hatch. A sign declared this to be the quarters of the *Titanic*'s lamp trimmers.

He banged against it with his fist. "Hello? Is anybody there?"

No reply. Instead, a deep groaning sound came from the other side of the bulkhead. Definitely not human.

Alfie twisted the wheel that operated the door — there was a little resistance — until it clicked. Then he pushed.

The hatch wouldn't budge.

The girls joined him, lending their slender shoulders to the task. It was as if some great weight were in the trimmers' quarters, holding the door fast.

At last, the steel hatch swung inward and a torrent of water exploded from the other side.

CHAPTER TWENTY-ONE

RMS *TITANIC*
MONDAY, APRIL 15, 1912, 12:00 MIDNIGHT

The violent flow washed over Alfie and the girls. The force took their feet out from under them and swept them along the passageway.

So great was their shock that they were carried thirty feet aft before realizing how cold the water was. Alfie slammed into a bulkhead and spread himself as wide as possible to spare the girls such a jarring impact. They slipped and slid around the bend until the torrent abated enough for them to regain their feet, sputtering and coughing. The flood ran along E Deck several inches deep.

"Paddy —" Juliana gurgled.

"Right!" Alfie gasped.

The three splashed their way to the master-at-arms' office. Water was streaming in the open door. The two cells at the rear of the room were occupied —

Paddy in one; Kevin Gilhooley and Seamus in the other. The sea was already at their ankles.

Gilhooley rattled the cage, bellowing for the master-at-arms in language the two young ladies had never heard in their lives.

"What's going on?" Paddy demanded. "What did we hit?"

"An iceberg," Alfie told him. "Where's Master-at-Arms King?"

"The crash knocked him right out of his chair, it did. Ran off like he was shot from a cannon."

"Cowardly git!" roared Gilhooley. "Leaving us here to drown!"

"But two big galoots throwing me overboard — that was fine and honorable!" Paddy retorted.

Sophie ran into the passageway. "Mr. King! Mr. King!"

There was no reply. The corridor was deserted, the inrushing sea pouring from the trimmers' hatch. She ran for Scotland Road. Surely there would be crew there.

The thoroughfare was crowded, but not with sailors. The third-class single men, quartered near the bow, were moving aft, carrying their possessions in hastily assembled bundles.

"Is an officer among you?" she asked anxiously.

"Oh, dozens," said one young Irishmen sarcastically. "And the bleeding Prince of Wales is there, too. Bailing, he is!"

An older man was kinder. "Don't go that way, miss. The holds are swamped, and steerage, too!"

Sophie spun on her heel and raced back to the brig. Progress was slow now, and the fabric of her sopping dress was weighing her down. "No master-at-arms, no crew at all!" she reported, her voice sounding desperate. "Before you know it, E Deck will be underwater!"

Alfie began to rummage through King's desk. "Where does Mr. King keep the keys?"

"On his belt, the fool!" growled Seamus.

"But surely there's another set!" Juliana persisted.

"Stand back!" ordered Alfie. He picked up the wooden chair, which had begun to float, and aimed a mighty blow at the door of Paddy's cell. The chair shattered, but the lock held.

"Find a fire ax!" cried Sophie, shivering as the water rose past her knees.

"We don't need it!" Paddy exclaimed urgently.

"What are you going to do?" cried Juliana, panic-stricken. "*Wish* yourself out?"

"Give me your hairpins!" Paddy ordered the girls.

"Our *hairpins*?"

Alfie thought back to his friend breaking into the Astors' trunk. For Paddy, a hairpin was as good as a key. "Do it!" he urged.

Without hesitation, both girls produced an assortment of pins in varying shapes and sizes, paying little attention as their upswept hair cascaded down around their shoulders.

Instantly, Paddy was all concentration. He selected a long gold pin and a short, flatter piece in mother-of-pearl. Pressing his face against the bars, he reached his fingers out of the cell, inserted his "tools" into the lock, and went to work, the muscles of his hands undulating beneath his skin.

Juliana's teeth began to chatter as the water swirled at her waist. "You'll never manage it!"

Despite the pressure, Paddy cast her a cheeky grin. "I may not be an accomplished gentleman, miss, but this is what I do."

There was a loud click and the door swung wide. Paddy sloshed out into the room.

"You haven't seen the last of me, wharf rat!" Gilhooley shouted from the other cell. "You'd best keep looking over your shoulder! Even if I die, remember, you'll die, too, one day! And I'll be waiting for you in hell!"

The threat was still echoing in their ears as they waded into the passageway.

The bottom five steps were completely submerged as Alfie, Paddy, Sophie, and Juliana dragged one another up the staircase across from the office.

Paddy brought up the rear, ushering the girls ahead of him. "I can't believe you came for me," he said in wonder.

"It's my fault you were arrested in the first place," Juliana declared.

Paddy's eyes were wide. "But I'm nothing to you! I'm nothing to anybody!"

Sophie turned on him, splashing Alfie in the process. "What a terrible thing to say! You're our friend!"

"And you'd do the same for us," Alfie added.

I would, you know, Paddy agreed silently. Before poor Daniel, Paddy had never even had a friend. Nor had he expected to have another after Daniel died. Yet here were these three, willing to brave icy water on a ship in distress in order to help him. What a time and place to discover there was something to live for!

Sophie felt her shivering abate as she cleared the fifth step. But her slippers still splashed in a thin trickle from above. "There's water on D Deck!" she breathed.

"That's impossible!" Alfie exclaimed.

"Then why is it coming down the stairs?"

"But —" All at once, Alfie had the answer. "The bow has taken on so much sea that the water-tight compartments are filling to the top! This is spillover!"

"But the ship can't actually sink," Juliana argued, "can it?"

Alfie repeated his father's words. "I think we're going to find out. It's a good thing we went for Paddy when we did. The brig will be swamped in no time. Hurry!"

The girls rushed ahead, but Paddy ground to a halt halfway up the flight, his expression inscrutable.

"Did you not hear me, Paddy? The bow is being pulled down! We've got to get higher and aft!"

"I can't leave them," said Paddy, speaking as much to himself as to the others.

"Leave *who*?" Alfie puffed.

"Gilhooley and Seamus."

The young steward goggled. "The *gangsters*?"

"I can't let them drown."

"Why ever not?" Alfie demanded. "They killed your friend! They nearly killed you! They *deserve* to be in that cell! Whatever misfortune befalls them there, they brought it upon themselves!"

Paddy nodded. "Right you are. They deserve to die. But not like this — not penned up like rats in a cage. That's no fate for anyone."

Alfie grabbed his friend by the shoulders. "Do you expect they'll show you gratitude for saving their lives? The moment you let them out, they'll murder you as soon as shake your hand!"

"Stay with the girls," Paddy told him. "Get them to safety. I'll come find you if I can." And he waded back into the flood that was inundating E Deck.

CHAPTER TWENTY-TWO

R·M·S *TITANIC*
MONDAY, APRIL 15, 1912, 12:09 A.M.

By the time Paddy reentered the master-at-arms' office, the water was lapping at his shoulders, and not much lower on the two prisoners.

"If you've come to watch us drown," Gilhooley sneered, "you might take stock of your runty self. You'll be kissing fish before we are!"

Without a word, Paddy reached for the hairpins he had pocketed. Drawing a deep breath, he ducked under and went to work on the lock on the second cell door.

Totally immersed in the frigid water, Paddy felt paralysis creeping over his muscles, hampering his movements. Salt stung his eyes, and he fought to keep them open, as he struggled to maneuver his cramping fingers. Lack of oxygen darkened his vision, and he broke to the surface, gasping for air.

He caught a glimpse of Gilhooley and his man star-
ing in utter disbelief that help should come from such
a quarter. But he cared nothing for them. It was not
Daniel's killers he was endeavoring to free. These
were two human lives.

Back underwater he plunged, trying to regain the
delicate touch that enabled him to navigate the guts
of the keyhole through the hairpins. Paddy had been
picking locks practically since the cradle. But never
before had he attempted the feat with numb hands,
burning eyes, and lungs starved for breath.

When he came up next, panting wildly, the water
was at his nostrils, and he had to stand on tiptoe,
sucking air. *Alfie's right*, he thought, his mind reel-
ing. *Why am I wasting precious time on these
worthless men? In another few minutes, the room
will be full to the ceiling. . . .*

Yet down he went once more, probing furiously. So
deadened by cold were his extremities that he almost
missed the silent click. In a single motion, he pulled
open the lock and straightened up to breathe. But just
as he was about to open his mouth, the awful realiza-
tion came to him.

I'm still underwater!

The office was awash over his head.

The panic was immediate and total. His brain begged for air, and he fought an impulse to inhale that screamed from every corner of his body and soul. Seawater in the lungs meant near-certain drowning. But if he couldn't breathe, he would surely pass out, which would achieve the same result.

The cell door was kicked wide, knocking him off his feet. He sprawled, part falling, part floating, until his shoulder struck something hard.

He forced his eyes open. The desk!

Delirious from oxygen deprivation, he struggled onto the desk. Blackness danced at the edges of his vision. He was passing out. . . .

No! Not when I'm so close . . .

Mustering what little strength he had left, Paddy pulled himself upright. His head broke the surface, and he wheezed hungrily, breathing in draft after draft of the sweetest air he would ever taste.

Barely eight inches separated the rising flood from the ceiling. Paddy could see Gilhooley and Seamus behind him, their heads bobbing as they struggled to swim out of the brig. Paddy filled his lungs once more and jumped off the desk. The salt water buoyed his weight, so that a few bounds carried him out of the office to the swamped staircase.

He scrambled up the steps until he was free of the water, splashing through the trickle toward D Deck. He had just made it to the top when Gilhooley's voice reached him.

"Lad — come back!"

Paddy kept on running. Come back? Not likely, and it wasn't just because the gangster and his henchman had already tried to murder him once on this voyage.

Maybe the White Star Line believed the *Titanic* was unsinkable, but Paddy knew better. Daniel had sketched out what might sink her. And Daniel was the smartest person Paddy had ever known.

The question was this: Had a mindless mass of floating ice somehow put the solution on Daniel's mysterious drawing into action?

There was no time to ponder that now. Paddy Burns had no formal education, but the streets of Belfast had been a course of study in the school of survival.

He had a feeling that the coming hours would test him like he'd never been tested before.

CHAPTER TWENTY-THREE

Cocooned in the first-class comforts of stateroom A-17, Robert Masterson had no idea that the *Titanic* was filling with water. A Deck seemed rock solid beneath him — indeed, more solid by far than the worthless legs that he used to stand upon it.

Besides, his mind was awhirl with the events on the forecastle. For the first time in twenty-four years, he had attempted to resume the work that had been interrupted by his accident. The fact that he had failed — alas, that was a technicality.

Jack the Ripper was reborn! And when the doctor in New York restored his legs . . .

His every impulse was to prowl the ship and finish what he'd started tonight. The young steward had already paid for his meddling with a broken head. What was left of him was going over the side. And that horrible girl with him.

But now was not the time. People were up and about, no doubt excited at seeing ice scattered about the deck. Weak-minded fools! To become overset by a silly iceberg when there were great matters afoot.

No, the stateroom was the right place for him at the present. If an officer came knocking at his door to investigate the girl's wild tale, he could claim he'd been here since dinner. It would be his word against hers, and she was a mere female. Everyone knew that women were vaporish and unreliable. And who would believe that a poor cripple could be guilty of attempted murder?

He settled back in an armchair. In an hour or two, all this excitement would die down. That was when he'd take his revenge.

Once more, the night would belong to Jack the Ripper.

EPILOGUE

RMS *TITANIC*
Monday, April 15, 1912, 12:09 a.m.

The *Titanic* lay at a dead stop in the Atlantic, her three active funnels bellowing as the great liner let off pent-up steam.

On the bridge, Captain Smith and Thomas Andrews returned from a quick sounding of the ship. Now they faced each other. Their quiet voices belied the shock and dread both men were feeling after their tour of inspection.

Smith checked the designer's hastily compiled notes. "We have water in the forepeak, both forward holds and mail room, and Number 5 and 6 Boiler Rooms. It's contained in five, but everything forward is flooded."

Andrews nodded grimly. "That would indicate a gash of" — he performed a mental calculation — "three hundred feet in length."

The captain looked into Andrews's eyes. "And this means . . . ?"

There was a brief flash of emotion in the ship-builder's normally placid gaze. "She can float with any two watertight compartments flooded. Even with three of the first five. She can survive a head-on collision that annihilates her first four compartments entirely." He squared his shoulders. "But what we have is the first five compartments ripped open and weighing us down. In time, the bow will sink so low that the fifth will overflow into the sixth, which will eventually overflow into the seventh, and so on. It is a mathematical certainty."

"What are you saying, man?"

Thomas Andrews drew in a deep breath. "The *Titanic* is doomed."

GORDON KORMAN

started writing novels when he was about the same age as the characters in this book, with his first novel, *This Can't Be Happening at Macdonald Hall!*, published when he was fourteen. Since then, his novels have sold millions of copies around the world. Most recently, he is the author of *Swindle*, *Zoobreak*, and *Framed*, the trilogies Island, Everest, Dive, and Kidnapped, and the series On the Run. His other novels include *No More Dead Dogs* and *Son of the Mob*. He lives in New York with his family, and can be found on the web at **www.gordonkorman.com**.